The *Faraway* Mountains

Radu Guiaşu

The
Faraway
Mountains

Addison & Highsmith

Addison & Highsmith Publishers

Las Vegas ◊ Chicago ◊ Palm Beach

Published in the United States of America by
Histria Books
7181 N. Hualapai Way, Ste. 130-86
Las Vegas, NV 89166 USA
HistriaBooks.com

Addison & Highsmith is an imprint of Histria Books. Titles published under the imprints of Histria Books are distributed worldwide.

Library of Congress Control Number: 2023939518

ISBN 978-1-59211-317-0 (hardcover)
ISBN 978-1-59211-333-0 (eBook)

To old friends

Author's Foreword

This novel started as a not-so-short story inspired by a hiking trip with good friends through the Apuseni Mountains of northwestern Romania in the summer of 1981, when I was eighteen years old. A few months later, at the beginning of 1982, I left Romania — the country where I was born and raised — and settled in Canada, where I have spent the majority of my life so far. During all the years I spent in Romania, I lived under a communist dictatorship.

The initial short story about the mountain climbing journey kept expanding as I continued to add more and more details and new stories, based mainly on my last year in Romania, but also on events, impressions, and memories from my childhood and adolescence — particularly the early school years.

Although the novel is clearly autobiographical, at least to some extent, this is still a work of fiction, which allowed me to expand the story beyond direct experiences and broaden the scope of the work. None of the characters in the book are based exactly on people I used to know, and the mountain climbing adventures are inspired by several trips to various Romanian mountain ranges during my youth: for example, the Bucegi, Făgăraș, Ciucaș, and the aforementioned Apuseni Mountains.

My love of mountains started early, and to this day, whenever I am near mountains, I feel happier. My parents have enjoyed hiking in the Carpathians since their university student days, and during almost every summer of my childhood, we spent at least a couple of weeks in the little mountain town of Bușteni, which remains one of my favorite places on Earth. This is where I first learned to appreciate the beauty of untamed nature, and this appreciation eventually led me to an academic career in biology with an emphasis on fields such as ecology, biogeography, and ethology. After I left Romania, I continued to explore mountains and beautiful natural landscapes in several countries, including Canada, Switzerland, Austria, and Norway.

This book describes a world that no longer exists — the Communist era in Eastern Europe in general, and Romania in particular. It is meant, at least in part, as a tribute to the special people who maintained their integrity, courage, and irreverent sense of humor despite the difficult conditions imposed on us by the dictatorship we lived under. The novel is also an indictment of all those who made our lives harder at the time by actively being part of, or collaborating with, the absurd repressive regime which governed our lives.

PART I
THE FARAWAY MOUNTAINS

1

From the top of the nearest peak, they must have looked identical and insignificant, like ants following each other on a scent trail, only their motion distinguishing them from the surrounding dirt.

They had started their ambitious ascent in the mid-afternoon. As they continued climbing steadily through the steep wooded valley, along the clear glacial waters of the small mountain stream, the decrepit wooden hut they had left behind dwindled to the size of a rust-colored bottle cap, before disappearing from view altogether behind one of the foothills. Until a few years ago, the old cabin could still serve as a reliable, though very rudimentary, overnight shelter for stranded hikers. But that was no longer the case — part of the roof was now missing, and what was left of the interior had been invaded by various types of mold and small rodents. The shack had been built in the 1950s, presumably for surveyors from the city. It was rumored they had come to assess the suitability of the area for the development of a fancy skiing resort. Later on, there was talk about the construction of a paved road through the cliffs, leading to a brand-new dam on the other side of the mountains, and the shelter was renovated in preparation for the arrival of the first team of workers. But neither the rumors nor the talk of grandiose projects ever amounted to anything, and few local people could even remember anymore what all the fuss had been about.

The mountains, which only a few hours earlier had looked so harmlessly alluring from the bottom of the valley, as if they had simply been painted on a giant bright blue canvas, now rose menacingly near and undeniably real on both sides of the trail, like the forbidding walls of a most formidable citadel that could only be entered at some considerable but still-hidden risk.

The fragrant spruce forest was slowly giving way to thick clumps of alpine grasses and small, twisted coniferous shrubs that clung stubbornly to the exposed grayish cliffs. Among the nearly-barren rocks, only a few tall, isolated trees re-mained, bravely standing alone, as the advanced sentries of the large tree army gathered below, on the gentler side of the slope, out of the reach of the harsh arctic wind.

The familiar cold wind that often circled the peaks, protecting them from the invasion of the forest, greeted the three silent hikers once again, as they moved past the uneven tree line, keeping a steady, disciplined pace. Experienced hikers don't talk much on their way up the mountain; the value of not wasting one's breath was quickly learned up here. A long, tough trek, planned to last for several days, was ahead, and their strength needed to be preserved until the end.

Besides, they had done a lot of talking already, first in the train that brought them to the village, and again as they crouched down on top of logs in the back of the old truck that brought them, haltingly, from the railway station to the foot of the mountains, along a poorly-maintained gravel road.

Until the distracting wind suddenly started blowing by their ears, each man could only hear his own accelerated heartbeat, pounding alarmingly hard and fast, with all the urgency that comes from a startled cardiovascular system trying to remember how to cope with a strenuous workout after too many sedentary months. As they walked briskly, in a single file up the narrowing path, they knew they had to reach the plateau high above well before sunset to set camp for the night. Another hour, perhaps, and they would get there, if only they could keep up the same unhesitating pace.

There would be plenty of time for pausing to admire the breathtaking scenery in the days to come. In the meantime, they had to focus solely on their immediate objective, since none of them relished the thought of putting up the tent, making a fire, and cooking dinner in fading light. They also wanted to put as much dis-tance as possible between themselves and the dark forest below before nightfall. The old-growth forest was beautiful during the daytime but increasingly menacing as the evening progressed and downright frightening at night, mostly due to the abundance of bears, wolves, lynx, and wild boar that still resided there.

The tallest of the three men was first on the trail. Taking advantage of his longer legs and somewhat lighter load, he seemed to be walking a bit faster and easier than the others. He was also the only one with decidedly long locks and a full beard — two attributes that were considered to be open acts of defiance, if not budding rebellion, at that time, in the increasingly isolated country surrounding the faraway mountains. Bringing up the rear, with a determined frown seemingly frozen on his prematurely mature face, was a dark-haired, muscular, square-shouldered, and rather stocky man, burdened by a very large backpack and fairly thick glasses. But the largest rucksack of all, and the one which contained the only tent, belonged to the man in the middle — an energetic redhead with a round face full of freckles, who seemed, at times, to be making a clear effort to get closer to the leader, while, at other times, he dropped farther back, getting slightly in the way of the perpetually frowning man behind him.

They were probably following one of the ancient trails once used by Dacian warriors to escape from the advancing Roman legions. Perhaps it was the same trail subsequently chosen by generations of outlaws during the many centuries which passed since most of the Romans had left, and the Dacians had adopted a version of the Latin language and made it their own. But the youthful hikers, in their rush towards the first destination of their young journey, were completely unaware of those coincidences.

2

They quickly set up the big, dark green tent on a flat bit of terrain, somewhat protected from the nasty eastern winds by a helpful nearby rocky outcrop. The soil was shallow there, and the hard granite rocks underneath made it impossible to knock the light metal support pegs around the tent fully into the ground. For additional safety, they carefully placed heavy rocks on top of and around each of the six main steel pegs. The tent gamely held its elevated dome-like shape, for the time being, but the hikers knew if a storm came, the heavy winds could probably blow their vital portable shelter all the way down into the valley below. They chose to avoid worrying openly about the weather, and they made a point of cavalierly dismissing the gathering dark clouds and unsettling distant rumblings of thunder as regular occurrences for that time of the year. In the mountains, the weather was very unpredictable anyway, especially at the end of the summer. One had to expect that and take the consequences.

"Otherwise, we would never leave our homes, and would slowly rot in the city," Alex — the taller, bearded man — said, and the others were quick to nod in agreement, although not very convincingly.

Still, during the simple dinner around the fire, Victor, usually the more cautious one, and the only member of the group with eyeglasses and an impressive handlebar mustache, couldn't help remarking:

"This flat corridor sure looks somewhat like the runway of a small airport, doesn't it? If this wind picks up some more, it will carry our tent away like a paper airplane."

"Not with us inside, old Vic. We've all gained a bit of weight lately. Especially Dan," said Alex reassuringly, before quickly changing the subject from the troubling uncertainty of possible upcoming dangers to the safe recollection of recent risks left behind. "Besides, if we survived that wild ride on the logs, on the back of that rickety museum piece they called a truck, we'll survive anything."

"It wasn't really that bad!" Dan, the somewhat-chubby redhead, interceded impatiently, acutely aware that taking a ride on that old truck had been entirely his idea, and slightly irritated about the unfair reference to his weight — he had only gained at most five pounds or so in the last year.

"Not that bad? You're joking, I hope. It was nothing less than hell on wheels. Three and a half wheels, as I recall. A moving death trap that left behind a trail of rust and broken parts. Can anyone explain to me how the engine stayed on? Was it the masking tape?"

"What masking tape?"

"A lot seems to have escaped you. If you would have troubled yourself to actually open your eyes and look in my direction once in a while, you might have noticed that I almost ended up under those giant dancing logs, several times, as the antediluvian wreck took some of those nasty hairpin turns on the way up. I mean, you couldn't tell until the last minute, each time, whether the infernal machine was going to make it around the corner, fall sideways, or roll backwards. After a while, I stopped caring and tried to prepare myself for anything. It wasn't easy to decide if being flattened by a log would be preferable to getting tossed out into the precipice or vice versa."

"In the end, nothing happened, of course. And we saved a lot of time," observed Dan, in defense of the museum piece.

"A minor miracle, no doubt. Have you ever heard an engine cough like that? Towards the end of the ride, I was beginning to think that the pitiful old thing might just blow up, and put us all out of our misery," said Alex. "Isn't there a more humane way of coming here? Like being dragged behind a wild horse, for instance? Couldn't we just rent a couple of mules or something?"

"I don't think I could ride a mule. Can you?" asked Dan.

"How hard can it be? And they would have to be more rational than that idiot who drove the truck."

"We should get ready, in case the storm comes this way — as it probably will," Victor reminded them, peering through his glasses and scanning the darkening sky, which seemed to press down on the mountains, making them appear a little smaller somehow.

"There's nothing more we can do now. The tent is up. Dinner is done. And we're alone up here, in the middle of nowhere. At least the rain should wash our dishes, if the bears don't lick them clean first. To hell with it, we're finally out here, surrounded by all this risky, untamed nature, and it's just too damn early to go to sleep. So, let's not sit here looking glum. Let's tell some 'mountain' jokes to pass the time," suggested Alex.

Everyone present knew "mountain" jokes were the ones they couldn't normally tell in the city, or on the train, or anywhere else where prying ears could be listening and anonymous reports could be prepared.

"What makes you think you can trust us?" said Dan.

"Well, old Vic looks pretty reliable, in that stodgy way of his, but you're right, I'm not entirely sure about you. To be frank, I was a bit suspicious even before you got us into that lousy truck," replied Alex.

"Maybe I can gain your trust with a first joke, then."

"I doubt it, but go ahead."

So, Dan started telling a new joke he had heard from his former girlfriend — the young woman who had recently left him, as a few others had done before. The lengthy joke went something like this: The opening of a new highway linking the capital with another major city is being officially celebrated. The organizers decided to give a prize to the driver of the one-thousandth car which will pass by their booth that day. After some time, a black Dacia, the one-thousandth car, is stopped for the prize-giving ceremony. Inside, there is a younger man (the driver), a younger woman beside him (his wife), and two elderly people in the back (his parents). The driver rolls down the car window with a frightened expression on his face and tells the policeman: "Oh, please don't arrest me for not having my driver's license, officer. I beg you." His wife helpfully intervenes: "Don't listen to him officer. He's drunk. He has been drinking all morning, ever since he got up.

He can't help it. He's an alcoholic." The old woman from the back seat screams: "I told you we shouldn't steal a black car. It's bad luck. Isn't it true?" And she elbows the old man beside her, who had been sleeping up to that point. The old man wakes up suddenly and asks in a sleepy, high-pitched voice: "Are we in Germany already?"

The punch line probably wouldn't make much sense to a Westerner. What was the big deal about a trip to Germany, after all? But back then, in the 1980s, in their rather remote corner of Eastern Europe, on the wrong side of the Iron Curtain, they all knew, instantly and without needing any explanations, that the trip had to be illegal — a desperate attempt to escape and emigrate. And it was also clearly understood that the people in the car were not planning to visit the GDR.

"Not bad, Danny, not bad. Mildly subversive, in fact. But I am a bit confused. Since when are the policemen giving away prizes around here?" was all the reluctant praise Alex could muster.

"Well, at least I tried," said Dan, somewhat relieved to have remembered the entire elaborate joke without any stumbles. "Do you have anything? Or are you just a critic?"

"I normally don't remember other people's jokes. I simply make up my own, when necessary. But all right, if you insist, I have an overheard one somewhere in the back of my mind. Your joke may only get you a slap on the wrist if you're lucky. But I believe in going for the jugular. Here's one that would probably land you in jail for quite a while. Or worse."

Alex stretched his long, strong legs, ran his right hand through his thick, light-brown mane, cleared his throat, and continued.

"Our fearless leader — the most beloved and revered son of the Earth (may he return to it soon), the genius of the Carpathians, and all that crap — took time out of his busy schedule to visit some dingy small town. Don't ask me why. Perhaps they were opening a new toilet paper factory, or just a new public toilet, or because of some other glorious occasion like that. Who really gives a damn, anyway? The main thing is, he was there, in all his diminutive splendor, and he received the five-gun salute from a local group of soldiers when he got there in the morning. So, a little old lady lining up for bread hears the gun noise, and asks a passer-by, 'Can you tell me what's going on, sonny? Why are they shooting?' He replies, 'Oh, it's because the president is visiting us today.' A few hours later, the president is getting ready to leave the little town. So, naturally, they decide to give him another five-gun salute, to make sure his departure is also suitably honored. By this time, the old lady has finally made it to the front of the line, and bought her stinking loaf of bread. When she hears the guns go off again, she seems a bit surprised, and so she asks a passer-by (maybe the same one as before — it was, after all, a very small town): 'I'm sorry to bother you sonny, but why are they shooting again?' The passer-by says, 'Well, you see, the president is now leaving.' The old lady ponders the news for a little while, and her bewilderment seems to deepen as she asks: 'You mean, they didn't get him the first time?'"

There were some nervous chuckles this time, and, even though they were indeed alone in the middle of nowhere, for a brief moment, they were instinctively more concerned with such irreverent lines being overheard by the wrong ears than with the approaching storm. Instead of relieving the tension, the joke managed to exacerbate it, somehow.

"That would never happen in real life, of course," sighed Dan. "He'll die of very old age many years from now, on his throne — probably long after I'm gone."

"And they call me negative. Let's keep some optimism, for crying out loud. Maybe you'll both go at the same time," observed Alex.

"There's no room for optimism here. We all walk around like zombies — heads down, lowered shoulders. Totally defeated and resigned. I will never see it, even if I live to be a hundred. Maybe in Hungary or Czechoslovakia, or wherever, but never here. The grip is just too tight," Dan continued.

"Who told you that zombies are defeated and resigned? If they were, they wouldn't be sinister, would they? Besides, even zombies may wake up eventually. The full moon, or whatever stimulus they respond to, will rise one day, the clouds will vanish, and the whole thing will blow up, like that wonder truck you loved so much almost did. Could be fun. Too bad I won't be around to enjoy the show," said Alex.

"Yeah, I feel really sorry for you… Poor you! I was just wondering how you'll manage to cope without seeing *his* face every day," said Dan with mock compassion resulting from obvious envy.

"I've seen *him* more than enough. His portrait hung in every classroom I've ever been in — too bad it was only his portrait. They always kept his perennially youthful image on the wall — never bothered to update it and show us what he really looks like today: old and edgy. His often-retouched picture is on the front page of every lousy newspaper, every stupid day, and most of what's left of our pitiful TV programming seems to revolve around him. I mean, how many factory visits does the guy have in him? How can he stand it? Can't he just stay home and read a book once in a while, or have someone read it to him, slowly? A nice, simple, short book, with few long words and lots and lots of pictures. You know: 'This is a hammer. This is a sickle…' — that sort of thing. Well, anyway, I think I am ready for detoxification."

"Did you ever actually see him? I mean, in person," asked Dan.

"Only once, for about ten seconds or less, as the motorcade went by. But we had to wait six hours for the privilege. I was still in elementary school, and they had us lining the boulevard on both sides, waving little flags on a horribly hot summer day — a real pavement-melting scorcher. My shoes were sticking to the gooey asphalt. It was the official visit of yet another little dictator from some other hellhole — I mean some other multilaterally developed society, of course. When the open car went by, they looked like two wax figures — lifeless and brainless. I was hoping they would melt. It seemed surreal. Nobody around was really cheering, so this secret policeman shoved me from behind and hissed in my ear: 'Why don't you shout 'Hooray!' young comrade? Show your patriotism and national pride!' Can you believe that? Young comrade? I was in grade six, for heaven's sake, the heat was unbearable, and I thought I was about to pass out from dehydration if the sunstroke didn't kill me first. All I could think about was ice-cold Pepsi coming out of a water fountain," Alex remembered.

"How do you know he was a secret policeman?" asked Dan.

"Was yesterday your first birthday? Who else would wear a heavy black leather jacket in mid-summer? And he had this stupid walkie-talkie he kept speaking into. Can you think of a store where you can buy those? You know, all those idiotic, nonsensical comments they make, just to show off. 'Alpha, bravo. Alpha, bravo, alpha. The toilet is leaking. I repeat, the toilet is leaking', or whatever the hell he was saying. It never makes any sense, but it doesn't matter, because the whole point is just to show the rest of us how many of them are there, ready to pounce if there's any hint of trouble. Just in case the motorcade is stormed by fed-up sixth graders with nothing to lose."

"If he were a real secret policeman, he would be saying 'The toilets is leaking, The toilets is leaking,'" observed Dan.

"Good point," conceded Alex. "As much as I hate to admit it, there may be some hope for you after all."

"So, judging by the conversation so far, it seems like you are beginning to finally trust me a bit," said Dan.

"Not necessarily. I forgot to mention that I went through your backpack earlier, while you were sleeping with your mouth open on the train, drooling on your shirt, and, since I couldn't find any tape recorders among your neatly folded clothes, I decided it would be safe to loosen up and tell you that gun salute joke," Alex replied. "Besides, you goaded me into it, as I recall. Victor is my witness. And should you ever tell on me, I'll just say that I initially heard the joke from you. Not to mention all the other really bad ones. By the way, your clothes are no longer neatly folded, of course."

"I never fold my clothes neatly," observed Dan.

"So, who did it for you, then? Was it your grandmother?"

"Let's leave the grandmothers out of this."

"What is it with all these restrictions? I'm in the middle of the freaking mountains, for crying out loud — at least here I should be able to speak freely," protested Alex.

And so they kept on going, arguing well into the night about such weighty topics as the future of the country (was there one?), the daily impositions of life under dictatorship (how much more absurd will they get?), the breathtaking stupidity of various high officials (was it genetic, or a job requirement, or both?), the continued decline in the standard of living (was there a bottom?), the shameful recent demolition of many architectural treasures (will there be anything left for future generations to appreciate?), the title race in the national football (known in North America as soccer) first division (was it all a sham, just like everything else?), the chances of finding someone who could lend them a copy of the latest Pink Floyd album (perhaps Alex's attractive fair-haired friend who worked as a stewardess on the international routes?), the recent prices of foreign-made blue jeans on the black market (could they possibly climb even higher in the future, or would it be wiser to wait a bit longer before buying?), the record heat wave they had left behind in the capital (would it still be there when they went back?), Dan's ongoing medical studies (would they bring him professional satisfaction in the long run or just utter despair?), Alex's future travel plans, the fantastic Swiss chocolates Dan had somehow managed to obtain and bring along for the trip (would they last for a few more days in the backpacks without melting in the heat of the day, or should they all be eaten now, just in case? Alex was in favor of the second option, but he was outvoted two to one, after which he opined that democracy also sucked, and may not be a satisfying alternative either), the quality of the stream water they had recently sampled, and exactly what concentration of cow urine dissolved in the water would be enough to give them some lifelong debilitating condition, and so on.

Victor, mostly quiet since his opening remarks, was not really listening to them. The increasingly wild wind was pushing the embers closer to the tent, and somebody had to keep an eye on the fire. Besides, he knew these topics all too well, and didn't feel the need to revisit them again. All those energetic speeches, all the futile worries and meaningless arguments, and all that youthful anger and harmless sarcasm wouldn't likely change anything anyway, except, perhaps, for contributing to future ulcers (Dan was already experiencing some symptoms) and premature gray hairs (Alex already had a few). It was like throwing pebbles against the fortified wall of a seemingly impenetrable bunker. There was nothing they could do to change anything. The future of the country, just like the weather or the prices of blue jeans on the black market, was entirely out of their control. They were just three young men far from home, in the middle of nowhere, always in constant danger of getting more or less lost. Or worse.

Furthermore, Victor was too busy observing the gathering dark clouds, and counting, each time, the seconds elapsed between the appearance of each flash of lightning and the corresponding sound of thunder. The intervals seemed to be getting progressively shorter.

3

That night, as Victor had feared, a violent storm descended over their tent and the valley below as they tried to sleep. The wind that had welcomed them only a few hours earlier was now gathering unsettling strength, and seemed to be offended by their continued presence on the mountain. The heavy rain, mixed with hail, was lashing the tent. Frequent lightning strikes cut through the darkness, illuminating the surroundings like a massive fireworks display.

"I didn't think anything could keep me up tonight," Alex said, now fully awake and fumbling in the dark for the flashlight, in order to better examine a possible leak through the ceiling of the tent. The suspected leak happened to be just above his head. "If we live through this storm, I should remember to switch places tomorrow night," he mumbled to himself.

"We're lucky we have these new, flexible fiberglass tent poles," Dan noted, sounding more hopeful than relieved. "The old tent, with those rigid metal poles, would never have held out for this long in a storm like this." It was Dan's modest way of reminding the others that the new tent was his and that they were probably all still alive now only because of the remarkable new gadgets he always brought along during these trips.

"This one won't hold forever either, if the storm doesn't let up soon. Besides, this is hardly the time for singing the praises of an unproven, brand-new tent. If it still stands tomorrow morning, then I'll join you for the chorus," offered Victor, bleakly, as the flexible poles kept bending more and more, seemingly in all directions, allowing the wet sides of the tent to hit the young men's faces, as they tried to keep their composure.

"It's a top-of-the-line tent," said Dan, feeling a bit stung by Victor's comments. "One of my father's well-connected patients brought it from a trip to Switzerland and gave it to him as a gift."

"All that stands between us and the unchained elements is this thin piece of fabric. Somehow, I don't find that reassuring," said Victor.

"For now, we're still better off inside the tent than out there, in the middle of that deluge. This is all we have, aside from our health. And if the tent does eventually get blown off this rocky ledge, well, at least we'll have a memorable last ride," concluded Alex, as a way of raising everyone's morale.

At that time, the memorable last ride did not seem all that unlikely. At least, if it had to happen, their demise would unfold in a beautiful place, surrounded by majestic mountains and deep forests, far away from the big city — with its perpetual gridlock and multi-layered, corrupt bureaucracies — where they had to spend most of the year. Their friends from the capital would always remember them, during lazy discussions in the coffee houses, for the spectacular, almost legendary, way in which they ended their hiking days.

4

Alone for a few days in Alex's apartment, Gabriel had the soothing feeling of finally having discovered a home he would have been glad to call his own. Aside from the magnificent old piano in the living room, the wall-to-wall and floor-to-ceiling wooden shelves, barely withstanding the weight of hundreds upon hundreds of wonderful books, immediately caught every visitor's eye. Gabriel — an avid reader and admirer of books — found the experience of being alone and surrounded by the works of so many good writers almost overwhelming.

"It's all here, old friend, from Albert Camus to Agatha Christie," Alex had told him proudly during his first visit to the apartment, in order to highlight the wide range of works on the shelves. Alex considered the distance between the bodies of work of his two chosen authors, both of whom he greatly admired, to be much greater than the alphabetical distance between their names, even though both distances were very difficult to quantify with scientific accuracy.

Ironically, Gabriel and Alex had initially been brought together by their shared inability to read. On the hectic very first day of elementary school, they were found to be the only two six-year-old boys who had skipped kindergarten and were entirely unable to read and write. As a result, they became school bench mates, and were placed behind the dreaded front desk of the central row so they could receive special attention from their teacher. The outnumbered boys, in their dreary black uniforms, were seated in pairs in the central row, flanked on both sides by the rows of girls' desks. The wobbly old desks and creaky benches were nailed to the floor of the crowded classroom, presumably to prevent anyone from walking away with them.

The nostalgia of the unanticipated memory of his first day of school made Gabriel smile, even though he had found that particular day to be very frightening

at the time. Somehow, the ill-fitting black uniforms seemed to indicate the inevitable loss of freedom to come. None of the kids appeared happy to be there, except
for one or two who were probably too slow to realize what was really happening
to them. Even Alex had wiped a lonely tear from his cheek with his father's all-
purpose tie.

A few months later, a new item was added to their already-depressing school
uniforms. They had to wear a rectangular arm patch — made of cloth and sewn
onto the coat of the uniform, which indicated the school number and the student
number. Their school was number fifty, and Gabriel was number 1239. This was
likely a way to keep tabs on pupils who misbehaved in public or were caught out
of classes during school hours. Presumably, anyone could report them by using the
numbers on their sleeves, even if they didn't know their names or anything else
about them.

As they entered the school building at the beginning of each day, usually drag-
ging their feet, a stern teacher stood beside the entrance to check if their uniforms,
including the numbered arm patches, were in order. Furthermore, a giant mirror
was placed in the corridor, near the entrance, supposedly so that students could
check their appearance on a regular basis. After a little while, someone drew a big
sad face, with the corners of the mouth pointing downward, on the annoying mirror. Even though the principal launched an urgent investigation into the scandalous incident, the culprit was never found.

But the chaos of the first few days of school soon gave way to the not-always-
unpleasant routine of lectures and assignments. By the end of the first term,
Gabriel started to enjoy his time in school a bit more, and Alex was at the top of
the class.

After the completion of grade one, Alex earned the first prize as the best student. He kept the diploma and the laurel wreath but, in one of his sudden acts of
kindness, he gave Gabriel one of the prize books — *The Magic Chalk* by Zinken
Hopp — as a gift. During his detention, Gabriel would sometimes dream of having a little Magic Chalk of his own, which he would use to draw the outline of a
simple door on one of the cold, damp walls of his small cell. And then, just like in
the first story he had ever read, the door would suddenly become real and open by

itself towards the forbidden outside world. If he had stayed with Anna, he might have been sailing along the peaceful deep waters of a wonderful fjord in Norway, Zinken Hopp's homeland, instead of ending up in a miserable jail cell, surrounded by the larger prison his country had become. But Anna was much too kind, beautiful, and generous, and he did not deserve her.

Alex and Gabriel remained bench mates for eight years, until the start of high school, without ever arguing. And they always backed each other during the inevitable fights against courtyard bullies and the occasional run-ins with the principal. At some point, in grade two or three, they became young pioneers, like all the other school kids of their age, and the mandatory red tie was added to their school uniform as a result. During breaks between classes, when no teachers or other adults were present, the children sometimes used to sing their own version of the young pioneers' song. They had changed the opening line, from the banal, "I have my own red tie, I'm a pioneer," to the more realistic and risky, "I have my own red tie, I'm a prisoner," which, at that age, seemed like the height of wit.

Another copy of the book received from Alex, all those years ago, was now before Gabriel, among the many other works. Although novels were in the majority, beautiful leather-bound volumes by some of Gabriel's favorite poets, such as Byron and Eminescu, and playwrights, from Caragiale to Ibsen, also had their places of honor on the sacred shelves. Beloved tales that had added so much joy to many a childhood (although, like all the best children's books, they were still meaningful for thoughtful adults) were also there, up on the top shelf, almost touching the ceiling. Hans Christian Andersen, who had first taught Gabriel that happy endings are not always essential, even for children's stories, Lewis Carroll and his quirky make-believe world of endless possibilities, the reassurance offered by A. A. Milne and Kenneth Grahame, and the delicate sadness from Antoine de Saint-Exupéry... Gabriel didn't know many details of these authors' lives, but he worshipped their names.

He remembered his mother reading *Le Petit Prince* to him when he was very, very young, before kissing him on the forehead and whispering: "Sleep well, my little prince." It was one of his few remaining memories of her. He was five years old when the car accident took away both of his parents forever. After that, his uncle, the engineer, took him in, and did the best he could, but nothing could heal the lifelong sadness left behind.

Gabriel had been a sickly child who missed school often because of various illnesses. Alex always visited during those times, brought Gabriel the lecture notes and various assignments, and sometimes even helped Gabriel with the homework — particularly the math-related work, which frequently gave Gabriel trouble. For some reason, Alex rarely became ill and seemed to have been endowed with a particularly robust constitution.

During his childhood, Gabriel did not have many friends and he wasn't very good at football, the predominant team sport for the boys in the playgrounds. Actually, he rarely touched the ball, and, when he did, he almost invariably sent it in the wrong direction. He never got much of a chance to learn the intricacies of the game, since he never got picked for any team, except for the times when Alex was team captain. Alex would always make room for Gabriel on the team, somehow, even for the important matches. Often, Alex could win a game almost by himself, despite Gabriel's glaring defensive liabilities. Gabriel appreciated his friend's well-meaning efforts to include him on those teams, but he knew he didn't really deserve to play, and therefore he started to stay away from the playground more and more often. During those times, alone in his room, he found refuge in the beloved books of his childhood. He didn't have too many, but he read each of them many times. He would always read them during lunch and supper, as well. Those well-worn books could still reveal much about his favorite foods during those years.

One of the middle shelves contained all of Jules Verne's many published works, arranged in the chronological order of their publication. How could anyone find the time and the energy to write and publish so much? Gabriel had travelled the known world and far beyond through many of those amazing books, eagerly navigating distant rivers and seas and exploring enchantingly mysterious faraway lands without having to leave his favorite creaky armchair and without needing to apply for an improbable passport and an even-less-probable visa. He had read somewhere that Jules Verne did not travel much either, in a strictly physical sense, beyond the limits of his hometown. Maybe this wasn't true, but even if it was, at least Jules Verne could have traveled more often, presumably, if he would have chosen to.

And there was so much more in between the exquisite antique marble bookends, shaped like miniature Doric columns, on each shelf. Respected works of literary criticism and philosophy published before the war. Rare collections of old sketches and modern Western comic books (good old *Pif* magazines and *Asterix* booklets — treasured mementos of Alex's not-too-distant childhood), side by side. The many scientific treatises that Gabriel respected, but felt he couldn't even hope to ever really begin to understand, occupied a very large bookcase covering an entire wall. Some of the names on the somehow-more-intimidating and severe-looking covers of the scientific volumes were very familiar indeed (for instance, Newton, Darwin, Einstein — the celebrated Beethovens of their respective fields, and some of their prominent predecessors, contemporaries, and many followers). But most of the sometimes-revolutionary findings that had given such an awe-inspiring aura to those names remained fairly mysterious to Gabriel, and for that, he felt a bit embarrassed and uneasy. His deep respect for knowledge and learning made him consider his own overall level of education as sadly inadequate on all fronts. This was one of the many attributes which set him apart from his tormentors, who displayed their complete ignorance of virtually everything worth knowing with a sort of bizarre, ostentatious pride. Alex used to call them, "the aggressively moronic."

Everything seemed to be available in this veritable readers' paradise. This vast magical library, improbably crammed inside the narrow walls of the relatively-small apartment, brought together the wisdom and the wit of some of the greatest authors the world had ever known, and held the exciting promise of many beautiful days spent trying to scale at least some of the authors' peaks of talent and imagination. Trying to decipher, understand, and imagine. All those great books, carefully gathered together, would have dwarfed any room and rendered any walls insignificant.

Gabriel had never seen so many books outside a public library. As an added bonus, like the prized dark chocolate figurine on top of the richest of birthday cakes, Alex's impressive book collection contained several titles which could not be found in any local public library. At the back of some of the lower shelves, in carefully concealed wooden toolboxes with misleading labels, buried underneath hammers and screwdrivers, were a few books smuggled in by Alex's brave airline hostess friend or brought by his parents from previous trips to the West. Solzhenitsyn's imposing *Gulag Archipelago* (all three monumentally thick volumes) couldn't have been easy to bring in, unlike the paperback version of the grim *A Day in the Life of Ivan Denisovitch*, which could easily fit even in a fairly small purse. Pasternak's epic *Doctor Zhivago* was also there, among the forbidden and officially frowned upon titles, together with banned works of philosophy, some of Alex's own carefully written unpublished manuscripts — typed, and with detailed handwritten notes on the side, and even a few issues of *Playboy* magazine. Only in a country like theirs, would (some) educated young men, such as Alex and his friends, long to read Solzhenitsyn's heavy books at least as much as they looked forward to peeking at playful magazines. The forbidden status elevated these works in their eyes almost as much as the translated words on the pages.

The special toolboxes, as well as the small Olivetti typewriter which Alex had somehow forgotten to register at the local police station, were hidden behind several, most likely carefully selected, older volumes. Gabriel knew this book arrangement could not have been coincidental. The books relied on to provide shelter for the boxes must have been among Alex's favorites. Gabriel examined the shelf, slowly and deliberately, from left to right, and smiled. Kafka's *The Trial* came first. Unlike Joseph K., Gabriel knew the crime he had been accused of, but couldn't quite understand why his actions would be considered criminal. Essentially, his only offence had been riding without a ticket. And that was simply because he couldn't purchase a ticket for his chosen destination. If only he would have been going in a different direction, towards an officially acceptable or pre-approved location, he most likely would have escaped only with a minor fine and a short sermon. A light slap on the wrist. But, as it turned out, that fateful ride had become the most expensive one of Gabriel's still-young life.

A thick tome Gabriel knew well, by Hašek, Kafka's compatriot, came next, shouldering the more fragile book to its left. Both Prague writers had died quite young, within one year of each other. For some reason, Gabriel had started to pay attention to the lifespan of some of his favorite authors. He noticed most of them hadn't lived very long or carefree lives. Even though Hašek and Kafka had passed away about six decades earlier, if they could have come back somehow, they would have recognized and understood Gabriel's predicament well. They would have been able to describe his plight and the absurdity of the world he lived in so much better than Gabriel felt he ever could. He might have been a compelling minor character in one of Hašek's bittersweet short stories. Yes, Hašek's satire was very much applicable to Gabriel's world. In the final analysis, it's said all dictatorships are essentially very similar in nature, regardless of the *Greater Cause* in whose name they claim to act. But in the myopic eyes of the thick-headed censors, Hašek was only a long-dead humorist, whose work belonged solely to the fairly distant past. To them, Hašek's cheerfully-delivered poisoned darts could only be aimed at the specific inanities of the defunct Austro-Hungarian empire. Publishers in the capital felt much more comfortable about the work of potentially controversial writers who had died long before the last World War (the longer the better). *The Good Soldier Schweik* was the book that had sustained Gabriel during his long time in the army. The only book any soldier should ever need.

Ilf and Petrov had also died young. Almost equally young. Their two best-known novels, *Twelve Chairs* and *The Golden Calf,* met Gabriel's gaze next. Gabriel couldn't understand how two writers could have managed to write novels together, as a team. Writers are such an egotistical lot. How on earth could two writers agree on the contents of one page, let alone an entire volume? How would they combine their ideas and split the credit, without killing each other first? Would the order of their names, on the front book cover, be simply alphabetical (in which case the Ilfs would always have an insurmountable advantage over the Petrovs), or would it somehow be related to the relative contributions to the text? And how would those contributions be objectively determined by two fiercely partisan and self-centered authors? At least Jacob and Wilhelm Grimm were brothers, and they only had to agree on editing the many folktales they collected.

Gabriel also didn't understand how Ilf and Petrov's biting, satirical accounts of the somewhat less-than-glorious side of the Soviet Union shortly after the Bolshevik revolution could have been published under communism in the authors' homeland. The publication of the two books in Russia made it easier for the publishers in Gabriel's own country to follow suit. Of course, the obligatory editorial note had been dutifully placed, as a disclaimer, ahead of each of the translated versions of the two texts. An anonymous editor (or group of editors?) took great pains to explain, in very categorical terms, that Ilf and Petrov were actually only making fun of those wretched, anti-social, leftover bourgeois relics who refused to integrate, morally and ideologically, into the "Glorious New Soviet Society."

This reminded Gabriel of an old joke: A tourist was visiting Moscow's Red Square — probably during Stalin's time, although there's no reason why this couldn't have also happened on Brezhnev's watch — and noticed two dead generals lying just outside the entrance to Lenin's tomb. "What happened to him?" asked the puzzled tourist, pointing towards one of the generals. "It was a tragic accident. He ate poisonous mushrooms," answered one of the guards at the tomb. "What about him? He has a bullet hole in his head," persisted the stubborn tourist, pointing towards the other general. "He refused to eat the mushrooms," said the soldier. Of course, the joke had been pure fantasy. In reality, murdered generals would never have been displayed in such a public place (especially near Lenin's tomb), and even if many dead officers would have been stacked up in a pile in the middle of the square, none of the passers-by would have stopped to look or asked any questions, and none of the soldiers would have offered any answers (especially truthful ones).

The more the editors insisted that Ilf and Petrov's only targets were the immoral enemies of communism (all enemies of communism had to be deeply immoral degenerates, of course), the more it seemed to Gabriel that the books were meant as a sweeping indictment, camouflaged under layers of humor, of the multilaterally developed shabbiness of life under the brand of dictatorship which had afflicted his corner of the world. It was clear to Gabriel that the authors' sympathies seemed to lie with the wretched relics. And the more he was instructed that Hašek's work could only apply specifically to one type of long-gone regime, the more universal that work became.

Papillon was there on that lower shelf too, of course. Gabriel and Alex had discussed that book on several occasions (even before the movie version with Steve

McQueen and Dustin Hoffman came out), and, each time, their admiration for Henri Charrière, the man who had written the true story, grew a little more. Alex mostly admired Papillon's indomitable spirit and inexhaustible willpower, and Gabriel primarily loved the triumphant happy ending of the story. Hard to believe that such a good ending could belong to such an amazing true story of a man's relentless fight for freedom. Lately, as Gabriel was becoming more and more tired and frail, he started to have more and more respect for Papillon's incredible stamina throughout the ordeal. Willpower alone was, unfortunately, not enough either for a successful escape or for properly dealing with the consequences of unsuccessful ones. Physical strength similar to that of Jean Valjean, Papillon's remarkable fictitious countryman, and favorable opportunities created by good fortune or the proper, mysterious alignment of the right stars were also necessary ingredients.

Yes, Gabriel recognized Alex's sense of irony behind that strategic book arrangement. Obviously, the books found in full view, on that lower shelf, were even more deeply subversive than those confined to the narrow space at the back of the bookcase.

The hiding of the (officially) controversial books had been more of a symbolic gesture, rather than a practical measure, of course. If any full-time, dedicated serfs of the system, sheltered and, at the same time, diminished by their official powers, would have really cared to look for such items, they could have easily found them, after ransacking the apartment. While the existence of such books should not be readily advertised in front of casual and unreliable visitors (as Victor used to say: "It's better not to remind fate of our weaknesses."), the presence of the toolboxes at the back of the shelves was designed to act more as a signal than a camouflage. They were actually supposed to indicate the special nature of the library to a select group of a few close friends and relatives. The toolboxes, as well as the choice of books on display, helped define the nature of the library owner and signal his views, sympathies, and commitments to all actual or potential members of the unofficial club.

The seemingly carefree satire found in some of the books on that telltale lower shelf was also only a pretend camouflage. At first glance, the humor was intended to sugar-coat the darts enclosed within the pages, but upon closer inspection, it only managed to make the darts sharper and, therefore, more penetrating.

But more importantly, perhaps, all those books, beyond all the messages and the various, temporary interpretations, had been very enjoyable. Often, while reading them, Gabriel caught himself simply following the gripping adventures of the characters, or laughing at some of the jokes, and forgetting all about the deeper meaning or the possible hidden messages or implications.

Gabriel was of the opinion (not at all uncommon among his peers) that, in the entire history of their troubled country, nothing good ever came from the East (he could never think of Ilf and Petrov, when he would be expressing such a categorical opinion). Genghis Khan's marauding hordes, the invading armies of many a sultan arriving under the flags of the mighty Ottoman Empire, the imported calamity of Soviet communism, and the bitter winter easterly winds had all swept over their relatively small, defenseless land from the dreaded East. As an understandable result, Gabriel's intellectual compass, like those of most of his friends, was always turning towards the glittering West, which seemed to hold so many promises and so many temptations. Perhaps even more promises and temptations than could be found in Alex's charmed book collection. Even the more recent worthy contributions of the East, such as the published writings of a few brave and successful authors, could only come to them via the West, since in their East, only one version of history was allowed to survive, and that was not the version found in Solzhenitsyn's books. Not surprisingly, given his courage and the impulsiveness of his youth, Gabriel had tried to follow his compass and head towards the bright promise of the West. But his naive compass had led him straight into the brutal embrace of the bestial border guards, who caught him while he was trying to escape, hidden among wooden crates, in an ordinary car of an endless freight train.

Papillon had managed to escape from Devil's Island, floating on a sac filled with coconuts, through rough, shark-infested waters, for days on end, toward freedom. In contrast, Gabriel felt foolish for not succeeding in his attempt to get away, within the relative safety of the anonymous train, over a fairly narrow strip of land covered with barbed wire, through a bunch of tired guards whose intelligence he didn't think much of. Perhaps, he would have been safer swimming among sharks in the vast open ocean.

Because he really cared so much for Anna, Gabriel did not want to take advantage of her generous offer of assistance. He couldn't stand the idea that anyone would think he only married her to leave his prison of a country. He wanted to do it on his own, and had it all figured out. After he managed to escape, and made something of himself, if Anna was still willing, they would get together then.

Alex was away for a week on vacation with his latest girlfriend, a very attractive third-year drama student. Gabriel had obtained permission to move in temporarily to practice his old music, and possibly compose a new piece, on Alex's much-travelled Viennese piano. In return, Gabriel had agreed to water the ferns and violets scattered around the apartment, fix Alex's broken bike, and feed Fortesque, a bizarre South American catfish, who was Alex's only pet. Gabriel felt fortunate to have negotiated such a favorable deal. Alex had often been notoriously protective of his privacy in the past, although he was always glad to lend quite a few of his precious books (and even some of the magazines and comics) to his most trusted friends.

Gabriel looked down at the historic piano, which had likely sat in many fancy households, in at least four different countries, before being acquired by Alex's grandfather in the 1930s. The history of the piano was told, at least in part, by the small but revealing golden metal plates left behind by various piano tuners during the past century and a half. The piano tuners were proud of their work, and they left engraved inscriptions advertising their identity, location, and the year when the tuning took place on these metal plates, which were carefully hidden inside the piano. The oldest plate had been placed there in 1835 in Vienna. Then, the piano travelled to Salzburg, Mozart's birthplace, and then to southern Germany and Slovenia, before finally arriving in their country in the early 1900s. This instrument went to all these wonderful places I'll never see, thought Gabriel as he gently caressed the piano keys without pressing them hard enough to elicit a sound.

That afternoon, Gabriel would have loved to take the time to read or re-read at least a few pages from one of the many books in Alex's personal library. Unfortunately, following his release, Gabriel's once-perfect eyesight had been deteriorating more and more. His eyes couldn't focus on a printed page for more than a few minutes at a time without becoming unbearably tired. The headaches seemed to be getting steadily worse, and much harder to tolerate as well. Since he could no longer read much, Gabriel picked up a copy of a treasured book, Camus' *The Outsider* (the last book found on Alex's revealing lower shelf), and simply held it tightly in his hand for a little while.

5

After the long train ride, they walked along the desolate main street of the village, navigating around the many potholes — the street looked like it had been hit by a meteor shower — and searching for something roughly equivalent to a restaurant or a bakery. Alex was starving, and, being a very persuasive fellow, he managed to convince the others that a meal in the village was just what they needed before starting their hiking trip. They all agreed it would be wise to save the food supplies in their backpacks for later.

The crisp mountain air no longer reached the center of the village. More of the majestic old spruce trees on the nearby slopes had been cut down in the last few years to make room for additional houses and an expanded paper mill. School children had been summoned, in the dying days of their summer vacation, to apply protective white paint to the lower parts of the trunks of the dead trees lining up the main street, and to sweep the dust from one side of the road to the other.

As the three friends walked by the quiet houses and the dead trees, they noticed with some sadness that the tiny, privately-owned homemade ice cream store was out of business. The building seemed abandoned. The old lady must have died or moved away. Perhaps to Italy, where, according to some rumors, she had a younger brother. She used to make the best vanilla ice cream they could ever remember tasting. Better than the ice cream available in any of the capital's few remaining fancy restaurants. Hers was one of the rare, family-owned small businesses in their country, and there often used to be long line-ups to get into this popular tiny establishment, whose reputation for excellence extended far beyond the limits of the village. Private businesses were regarded with deep suspicion and usually not allowed by the communist authorities, since they reminded them of the country's still-not-too-distant capitalist past, which was negatively portrayed in the rewritten history books.

Despite the increasing signs of ugly encroaching urbanization, the village retained some of its old rhythms and traditions. Although many of the younger people worked in the paper mill and had abandoned a way of life based on small-scale farming, some houses still had attached stables, and old women could be seen taking the cows to rich pastures up the surrounding hills. There were relatively few old men around — many men had been killed prematurely by alcohol or work-related accidents, so most of the old women were widows.

After a surprisingly long walk (the village seemed to have gotten quite a bit bigger since their last visit), they finally stumbled upon an out-of-the-way, state-owned tavern, which was only distinguishable from the adjacent warehouses by the faded sign above the main door.

"I don't know about this place. It sort of frightens me," said Victor, eyeing the dusty sign and the overly-full garbage cans in front of the door with what could best be described as suspicion.

"It's either this place or the workers' club. And you've just seen the workers' club…" said Alex.

"Okay, enough said, let's go in," Victor decided.

To their surprise, the empty main dining room was actually fairly clean and pleasant. After a ten-minute wait, an attractive young woman, wearing an immaculate white apron over some sort of blue uniform, finally approached them, cautiously.

"Are you fellows blood donors?" she asked politely.

"Pardon?" was all Alex could think of replying.

"You see, today is Blood Donor Day, and we can only serve meals to people who donated blood in our clinic in the last month."

Alex felt like adding, no wonder the place is packed with happy customers, but, seeing the young woman's innocent smile, he restrained himself and simply asked, "Could you please tell us where we could get something to eat around here? We've been travelling on the overnight train and we're sort of running out of energy."

"You can always try eating on our terrace, at the back. That's where most people go, anyway."

"Wonderful. Thank you very much."

The gaze of the pleasant young woman followed them as they left the dining room and headed for the terrace. However, the indoor terrace fell quite a bit short, even of their modest expectations. A few long tables, covered with empty beer and liquor bottles, as well as the heavy heads of many of the sleeping drunken regulars, stretched across the rotting planks of the patio.

"Ain't the working class simply glorious?" Alex remarked, mischievously raising his left eyebrow. His normally powerful voice was barely audible among the shockingly loud snoring and burping noises all around. From the entrance, the squalid tables were hard to see through the curtain of thick smoke emanating from the dozens of burning cheap, filterless cigarettes. For some reason, the cigarette packs were labelled with the name of the country's main mountain chain. The link between cigarettes and clean mountain air did not seem obvious, and Alex thought the label on the packs of cigarettes must have been the result of sarcasm. The gray smoke and colorless liquor vapors seemed to have replaced most of the regular, breathable air, and were now the main gases in the room. After a lengthy search, the young men managed to round up three empty and relatively clean stools, which somehow had escaped from being vomited on, and they positioned themselves strategically at the head of one of the tables, close to the kitchen door. A not-so-faint smell of raw sewage and stale grease came in each time the door opened.

An openly hostile old woman, wearing an apron which would have been considered dirty even in a slaughterhouse, approached them slowly, swinging her enormous pachydermatous hips. A burning cigarette butt was hanging nonchalantly from a corner of her mouth, looking like it had been glued to her lower lip. She stopped in front of them and gave them a fierce look.

"Yeah?" she challenged them.

But Alex was too tough to be intimidated by the old woman's sour demeanor.

"Do you have a menu, please?"

"I can tell you what we got, if you need to know."

"Yes, please, I really need to know."

"Suit yourself, young man. We got Pork One, Pork Two, and Pork Three dishes today. And we're out of beer. I'll be back later to take your order, in case you decide to stay."

The old woman turned around and walked back, in slow motion, into the revolting kitchen, apparently indifferent to the puzzled looks on the young men's faces.

"What the hell is Pork Three?" asked Alex, choosing to focus his question, at random, on one of the items on the verbal "menu," even though he was just as confused about the precise meaning of Pork One and Pork Two.

"I don't know. Maybe the tail and the feet? Or the snout and the teeth? I told you this place frightens me," said Victor.

"It's not clear if Pork Three is the worst or the best in their hierarchy. I mean, is Pork One really number one on their list, in terms of relative quality, or are they counting increasing value from top to bottom, in which case Pork Three should be the best?" Dan wondered, while showcasing his analytical skills.

"Either way, just don't choose Pork Two," said Victor, extracting the main conclusion from Dan's analysis.

"Maybe there's no hierarchy. They're probably all equally repugnant. But, for the moment, I don't care if Pork Three is really baked pig excrement. I'm hungry, damn it, and I'm desperate enough to take a chance," said Alex, jokingly pounding the table with his fist. The vibrations caused by the banging of the fist on the cracked wooden surface failed to elicit any visible signs of life from the sleeping heads unconsciously lined up at the other end of the long table.

"Brave words, my unwise friend," retorted Victor, deliberately borrowing one of Alex's typical expressions. "Then again, I don't remember ever seeing you get ill on any of our trips. What's wrong with you? You must have the stomach of a shark."

"I told you, I was found as a baby in the wreckage of that spaceship," said Alex. "My home planet must have been a lot tougher than this one, incredibly enough."

In the end, they each ordered, deliberately, a different type of pork. "This way we can see which one is the least unappealing, and share that one," suggested Alex.

But, unfortunately, their brilliant strategy did not work, since all three dishes looked equally gray and smelled equally bad. To their unrefined urban taste buds, Pork One, Two, and Three seemed identical. The nasty, crabby old woman had clearly outsmarted them.

"Never underestimate your opponents, next time," cautioned Victor.

After some initial hesitation, they nibbled a bit on some of the softer, chewable potatoes, and then, after also seeing a big brown rat run into the kitchen through a hole at the bottom of the door, they left the tavern fairly quickly — and without looking back. Although they had barely touched their so-called food, they were clearly not hungry anymore. Dan, who had nibbled on one more dry potato than the others, was suddenly unbearably thirsty. With their appetite long gone, they could now concentrate exclusively on the first leg of their journey.

6

It was a glorious early morning — peaceful and bright, without a single cloud in the brilliant blue sky, and perfect for a rewarding walk. The only clear evidence of the intense storm of the previous night was the still smoldering, charred trunk of an old pine tree, which had been hit by lightning just a few hours earlier. It was the tree closest to the tent. A small grass fire appeared to have burned for a brief period around the remains of the tree, but it had petered out, mercifully, well before it could pose any real danger. That wasn't too far away... Not a good sign. Sooner or later, in one of these crazy trips — maybe even during this one, our luck is bound to run out, thought Victor, who was the first one to emerge from the tent that morning, looking for a place to pee. And yet, despite his ever-present concerns, as he relieved the pressure on his previously overly-full bladder behind a nearby boulder, he knew very well that, deep down, he was happy to be there. In fact, at that moment, he could not think of a better place to be. Being surrounded by such a dramatically beautiful landscape and all that fresh invigorating air, in the company of good friends, was a privilege many people never experienced, or didn't experience often enough. Such moments should be treasured and every detail should be carefully remembered, so that the precious memories could last longer and make other days — days full of frustration and disappointments — more bearable in the future. The coffee rarely tasted better, and even the now partially wet biscuits did not seem all that bad. Easier to chew, in fact. It was fantastic to be alive on a day like this, and the storm that had passed made Victor feel even more grateful for the opportunity to enjoy another fine morning. Who knew how many more would be left...

After a frugal breakfast, they set out across the plateau with their bulging rucksacks on their backs, against a stiff wind, but, nevertheless, happy and surprisingly fresh after the sleepless night. There was nothing like surviving a bad storm in the mountains to get the journey started on the right note. After all that rain, the air seemed even cleaner than before, and the high humidity enhanced the pleasant fragrances of the conifers, the grasses, and the flowers.

Alex started whistling the opening sequence to Johann Strauss' upbeat *Radetzky March*, and the others instinctively adjusted their walking patterns to follow the cadence of his energetic whistling. It was an easy rhythm to march to, and, on a morning like that, even marching could seem enjoyable, for a little while. The sounds reverberated through the narrow alpine meadow they were crossing, and they felt utterly alone, healthy, strong, young, and free to roam through their very own small piece of paradise. They had earned the right to be up there and enjoy the spectacular view. It seemed like nature was putting on a private show just for them, as a reward, perhaps, for all their effort and endurance, and for having survived the storm.

The huge shadow of a golden eagle passed over them, and they all looked up just in time to see the majestic bird of prey glide gracefully over the valley below. It was probably one of the last few golden eagles left in the wild, since this was an endangered species in these parts. It was even possible they were seeing the very last eagle left. They knew that soon, these magnificent birds may well pass into oblivion like the aurochs and other extinct endemic animals, and the next generation may only see them in books, or on postage stamps, or stuffed and on display at the Natural History Museum in the capital. However, this eagle was still here, in the wild and very much alive, and as long as these mountains remained largely unoccupied by people, there was hope for the other local species as well. Despite the dangers associated with the presence of large predators, such as bears or wolves, it felt good to know all this wilderness was still available in the late twentieth century, in Europe. One could travel for days through these mountains and never run into another human being. Anyone who thought their old continent was too crowded with people and too cluttered with settlements should come up here and look around. They had needed many hours to walk from the bottom of the valley to their current elevated location, and they watched with unbridled admiration as the eagle effortlessly covered that same distance in mere seconds without even moving its wings.

Even though they had all hiked in these mountains before, it seemed for a little while that this was the very first time again. Twin waterfalls came down the smooth cliff wall to the north of the meadow, carelessly spraying countless droplets of water in the wind, and the cool, soothing mist temporarily enveloped the hikers as they walked by, contributing to their growing sense of pleasant detachment. At that moment, they appeared to be the only members of their species present on the mountain. There were no sounds, no smells, no tracks, and no other sights which could have contradicted that assessment.

7

The illusion did not last long. Soon after they had rounded the imposing cliff wall, the faint sounds of small bells and barking dogs alerted them to the nearby presence of sheep and shepherds. Before they had enough time to analyze the new information, they saw two huge white sheepdogs with spiky metal collars rushing towards them. The hikers knew these dogs did not take kindly to intruding strangers, and were perfectly capable of tearing the odd tourist apart now and then. There were always rumors that the shepherds deliberately put hot peppers in the dogs' food or kept them hungry for days at a time, just to make them meaner. Those rumors seemed more and more plausible to the hikers as they watched the fast-approaching dogs come downhill to greet them. Soon, two more equally large dogs joined the frontal assault.

"Oh good, at first I thought we might actually have a fighting chance," said Alex, reaching for his hunting knife.

"Just keep perfectly still, and we should be fine. We've seen this before," Victor sensibly advised, trying to appear in control.

"If that fails to pacify them, I say we get back-to-back and show these oversized mutts what we're made of!" continued Alex, true to his notoriously feisty nature. He thought this might not be a good time to remind his friends that sometimes, shepherds who were either drunk or half-crazed after being alone in the mountains for too long, or both, would deliberately set their dogs on unsuspecting hikers from the city, for a lark. Sources of amusement were few and far between in the life of a lonely shepherd.

All the dogs stopped at the same time, as if they were all listening to an unheard signal, and surrounded the hikers. The big dogs were neither overtly menacing nor friendly. They seemed to be waiting. The men had little choice but to wait with them. They could see some barely healed scars on the bodies of some of the dogs.

These scars were probably the inevitable result of recent attacks by a marauding bear with a craving for fresh sheep flesh. Apparently, the berry crop had been unusually poor that season, and thus the bears were now coming for the sheep more often than usual. The shepherds in these parts were not allowed to carry firearms, so they had to confront the hungry bears armed only with long wooden poles and surrounded by their trusted five or six sheepdogs. It was a rough way to make a living.

After several tension-filled minutes, the shepherd finally arrived, fairly cheerful, perhaps a little drunk, and chewing indolently on a long grass stem. He was probably in his late thirties or early forties, although relentless long-term exposure to the elements had turned his skin leathery and made him look older. He was wearing a traditional small, round, black hat and a long sheepskin coat, Instead of the more traditional panpipe, a half-empty bottle of strong plum brandy was sticking out of his vest pocket.

He was speaking a strange form of the local dialect, which none of the young men understood very well since they had all been raised and educated in the faraway capital. The shepherd appeared to be used to having to repeat himself, however, and he did not seem to mind the occasional misunderstandings. He told them he had already lost six sheep that summer to his old nemesis, a crafty old bruin with a missing eye. They had played this game for about fifteen years already, and the bruin always got his sheep in the end. The shepherd's job, under the circumstances, was to minimize the losses. The villagers, a spiteful and ungrateful lot, were not always pleased with his work. They had repeatedly accused him of drinking and sleeping too much. Those kinds of unsubstantiated allegations could drive a lesser man to drink. But he had to remain vigilant. After all, his own livelihood and, possibly, his own survival were constantly at stake up here. Let those fat cats in the village come up here and take his place, if they didn't like the way in which he went about his business. They would never dare to come, of course, they just liked using him as a scapegoat, those wretched souls, may they all rot in the hottest part of hell.

Alex took an instant liking to the shepherd, and suggested that the villagers were probably jealous of the noble freedom of a shepherd's life. Free to walk around all summer long on those beautiful mountain pastures, high above the cramped little village the others were stuck in. Upon hearing this, the shepherd's face brightened. He hadn't considered it before, he said, putting his arm around Alex's broad shoulders in a brotherly fashion, but come to think of it, that was probably the reason for his constant persecution at the hands of those idiotic peasants. The poor bastards were simply green with envy.

Then Victor asked about the bear. How big was it? Did it ever attack people? And what was the extent of its territory?

The shepherd scratched his chin and said he couldn't be sure if the bear had ever killed any tourists, but it was certainly possible. A few years ago, a young fellow from the city insisted on going into these mountains by himself, for a day hike, and nobody ever saw him again. They found one of his shoes in an abandoned bear's den a year or two later. It was not clear exactly how it got there. They recognized the shoe, because it was some strange type of red tennis shoe, and you don't see that every day — in fact, you never see that around here, and everyone thought the young man was crazy, both for hiking all alone and, especially, for having red tennis shoes. Sure, the bear could have gotten him all right. This was no ordinary bear. He was huge, and cunning, and amazingly strong, and once broke the back of a cow with a single swipe of his giant paw, and after that he dragged the dead cow by the neck up a steep hill while some local farm workers watched in amazement, too stunned to move. But it was very unlikely the bear would decide to kill three tourists at the same time, the shepherd added, so there was probably nothing to worry about.

"Just don't get separated," he advised, and then slapped Victor on the back.

In the end, the young men bought some fresh sweet cheese from the lonely shepherd, shared a gut-cleansing drink with him, which they instantly regretted, and then went on their way.

A bit later on, they came across some distinctive, large, fresh brown bear tracks in the mud, and decided to put some more distance between themselves and the shepherd's hut and the sheep enclosure before setting camp.

8

When Gabriel finally came to, after the first round of severe beatings, he found himself tied to a simple metal chair, in what looked like a sparsely furnished office, without windows. Through his half-closed left eye (his right eye had become sealed shut under the repeated blows received during the night), he could barely detect the blurred outline of a corpulent middle-aged man, who seemed to be sweating profusely, despite the obvious chill in the room. Gabriel could not remember ever feeling this cold before. His toes felt numb and his head felt like an open wound. On the small table in front of him, Gabriel saw nothing but the contour of a large inkwell. If they wanted him to sign a confession, or something along those lines, they should have also provided him with a fountain pen, he thought, trying to avoid falling into a deep sleep again.

The outline of the smelly, fat man (Alex would have said the bloated son of a bitch was too busy torturing people to have time for a shower) was speaking to him, in an agitated manner, but Gabriel could not make out most of the words. Why would the bulky policeman appear so nervous and uneasy in front of a defenseless, injured student tied to a chair? Was the officer's eerie anxiety caused by a small, reactivated remnant of a dormant conscience, or was it merely a part of the cruel frenzy associated with the brutal interrogation? (Alex would certainly have chosen the latter).

Perhaps the torturer's nerves had nothing to do with the interrogation. After all, as a member of the security forces, the policeman must have been quite experienced at efficiently and methodically inflicting pain on others, and he was most likely immune to his victims' suffering. His main concern, fueled by his supervisors' approval, must have been the customary removal of all layers of dignity from each prisoner. That kind of job obviously required a special brand of individual — a sadist, paid by the state to give in to his most brutal and cruel tendencies.

Gabriel's tormentor was probably more concerned about his mistress's threats, or his wife's affairs, or even the heartburn raging out of control after his intemperate huge meals, than about the precarious state of Gabriel's health. Why did they react so violently towards a young man who was only following his youthful compass, quietly and on his own? Were they really that afraid and was their belief in the strength of their absolute power really so fragile?

Finally, there was a brief period of much-needed silence. A peaceful respite. For some unfathomable reason, Gabriel's thoughts turned to a clear mountain stream he had once crossed, a long time ago. The soothing cool water rushed over his tired muscles, and, as he looked down, he thought he could see his own shadow, floating on the surface of the water and stretching calmly behind him. The shadow seemed to be moving gently downstream, away from his exhausted body. He wondered how long it would take the shadow to glide, along cool rivers and across smaller seas, all the way to the welcoming warm waters of the Mediterranean.

Anna was there, on the other side, waiting for him. Although he turned to look at her, he couldn't make out all of her delicate features at once. He wanted so desperately to remember her entire beautiful face, but he could only recall fragments of it. The appealing gentle curve of a perfect eyebrow. The brilliant blue color of her friendly, trusting eyes. The changing shape of her mouth, as it opened into a delighted smile. The freckles and the dimples. No matter how hard he tried, he could only gather a few pieces of the elusive puzzle at a time. Her dear face remained an incomplete mosaic, and he felt the water getting colder and the current becoming stronger and harder to struggle against.

His brief escape across the stream was suddenly shattered by a heavy blow to the head, which led to an immediate explosion of pain. The hit seemed even harder than those administered by the border guards' boots. Through his badly injured left eye, in the brief moment before passing out again, Gabriel noticed that the large inkwell was no longer sitting on the small metal table.

9

That night, around the warm, reassuring fire, they started telling some of their favorite bear stories.

"It was the summer following the end of high school," Alex began, "you remember the euphoria and the relief, right after we found out we had passed all those tough, make-or-break university entrance exams. After one full year of constantly studying and worrying, suddenly, the exams were behind us, and we had the illusion of temporary freedom."

"Actually, for me it was more like two years," observed Dan.

"There you go, for some it was a two-year sentence — that's what you get for choosing medicine," Alex continued. "So, naturally, after all that work, we were all looking to get away from the city for a while. Some of the lazy ones went to the trendy and expensive seaside resorts to get fat and fry on the beach like stranded jellyfish — isn't that right, Danny boy? — but, luckily, a few of us always stayed loyal to the mountains. I couldn't find Vic — I don't know where you went..."

"Silvia's father needed me to help him renovate his cottage," said Victor, looking uncomfortable.

"Ah, really sorry to hear that," said Alex. "Fortunately, Gabriel was around, so the two of us went on a memorable, five-day trip through the southern mountain chain that July. Both of us had just broken up with our respective girlfriends earlier that month — the final farewell to the high school years, I guess. To be honest, I felt enormously relieved about this, or so I thought at the time, while Gabriel was sad, or so it appeared. Then again, you know Gabriel. He was often sad, but he kept his troubles to himself, and he was a true friend, always reliable and always ready to join any adventure."

"I didn't know him quite as well as you did, but he was always a great friend to me, as well," added Victor.

"A gentle and noble soul, indeed. One of a kind," Alex nodded, after a brief pause, before resuming his story. "In any case, the trip had been an unqualified success. We met most of our objectives — climbed all the peaks we had planned to reach and saw all the landmarks we wanted to see, and the weather had been perfect — the kind of steady good weather you can only dream of in the mountains. Nothing but blue skies all the way. So, encouraged by all that, and with a bit of extra time at our disposal, during our last full day on the mountain, as a bonus, we decided to take a small detour to a little-known glacial lake neither of us had visited before. We had been told there was an old, abandoned forestry road that led straight to the lake, and we went that way, since it seemed like a convenient shortcut, even though the route was not described in any of my guidebooks and not shown on any maps. It was obvious, judging by the condition of that road, which was barely visible under a dense cover of overgrown weeds and emerging shrubs, that no hikers had used it for a long time. I think there was even some sort of barrier blocking the path at one point, but we ignored it, of course, and went around it."

"Shortcuts can be deadly, I tell you," Dan heard himself say, for no clear reason other than to show that he was indeed following the story and anticipating the trouble ahead.

Alex looked at him, a bit surprised, and paused for a few significant seconds, just to make Dan squirm a bit, before continuing: "The hike to the lake was uneventful, but, on our way back, we suddenly heard loud noises of breaking branches and snapping twigs coming from our right — just above the trail. At that very moment, I detected the unmistakable smell of bear. It just hit me. I suddenly remembered smelling that very same type of distinctive odor as a kid, when I was standing very close to the bear enclosure at the alpine zoo. I never would have guessed the memory of this odd and rare scent would persist, well-hidden up to that point, for so long. They say humans have a very poor sense of smell in comparison with most other mammals, so I knew that, since I could smell the bear, it had to be very close to us. Without uttering a word, I turned around slowly in order to face Gabriel, who was walking right behind me. He looked quite concerned, and rather pale, as he said to me, 'You probably won't believe this, but I think I can actually smell a bear.' That independent confirmation of my own suspicion convinced me we were probably in serious trouble. Nobody could come to our rescue on that isolated road, several kilometers away from the nearest mountain hut. Before I could expand on my concerns, we heard the scary sounds of heavy approaching footsteps — much heavier than those of any human — coming once again from somewhere among the shrubs to our right. It sounded as if a clumsy, flat-footed giant was advancing towards us. I thought, since we could smell the bear with our relatively poor olfactory sense, the bear, whose excellent sense of smell is comparable to that of bloodhounds, must surely have detected our presence long before. After all, we hadn't had a proper shower in a few days. I knew bears are usually supposed to stay away from people, at least according to the experts. At the time, it appeared obvious to me that, since this bear did not seem to have any intention of avoiding us, it must have thought of us either as intruders in its territory or as main courses for lunch. Neither alternative seemed good, and I just kept waiting for the inevitable to take place, while holding on tightly to my alpenstock."

"That must have been quite intense. You never told me this before," said Victor.

"It's not easy to recall this even now. Especially here, in bear country. I'll probably need years of future therapy sessions to fully recover. Besides, it wasn't really one of my proudest moments, as you'll soon find out," said Alex.

"So, what happened?" asked Dan.

"Well, after the longest few seconds of my life, as I had anticipated, with a clear sense of dread, the bear did indeed come out from behind the shrubbery, and strolled slowly and cautiously to the middle of the path we had been walking on, essentially blocking our way. It seemed huge — it *was* huge, and, due to its dark brown color and impressive size, it reminded me, in a strange way, of my old Viennese piano. Except for the giant sharp, curved claws, the large muscular hump on its back, and the big teeth, that is. Come to think of it, I don't remember if I clearly saw either its claws or its teeth, but I am sure they must have been enormous. It was as if a nightmare was unfolding right before my eyes, and I couldn't believe I was really there and this was really happening. The bear was only about twenty meters in front of us — maybe even less, when it slowly turned its head and looked at me, seemingly with utter indifference. I'll never forget those blood-shot eyes, however. It must have known full well that it was in total control of the situation. I felt utterly helpless, and I really hated that feeling. The bear could easily outrun us, and it was obviously much stronger than any human, so there was really not much we could do. I couldn't move at all — only my eyes and my brain seemed still alive. They say that standing still is the right first step when running into a bear, but I didn't do this on purpose, believe me. Quite frankly, I was paralyzed by fear."

"Coming from you, that is quite an admission. In all the years I've known you, I don't think I've ever seen you show fear or admit to having experienced it," said Victor.

"We all experience fear sometimes, but we can choose not to advertise it. In this case, not doing anything may have saved my life," Alex confessed.

"Go on, finish the story," said Dan.

"My next thought, as I was standing there frozen, facing the bear, does not exactly fill me with pride, in retrospect. I don't know why I feel the need for full disclosure right now. It may have something to do with being up here, maybe for the last time. It could be the guilt I felt since then. Who knows? Keep in mind the extreme circumstances, before you judge me too harshly… There was a small creek below the path, to our left, and I thought that if the bear charged, my only chance would be to dump my heavy backpack on its head. Then, taking advantage of this diversion, I thought about quickly crossing the creek and climbing a tree, leaving Gabriel to fend for himself. Perhaps, the bear would become satiated after feasting on old Gabe. It's terrible, but fortunately, we'll never know whether or not I actu-ally would have done all that, or any of that, since the bear had the good sense to quietly walk down to the creek and leave us alone."

"Just like that?" asked Dan, incredulously.

"Just like that. You seem disappointed. Were you expecting blood and gore? You already knew we survived."

"Well, it is a bear story," said Dan, defensively.

"My bear story ends well," said Alex, trying to wrap up the tale properly. "Anyway, like I said, I'm not proud of it. I didn't really want anything bad to take place, of course, but, for a moment or two, I thought, well, if something horrible had to happen to one of us, it would be preferable if it didn't happen to me. The hike to the lake took us about two hours, but after seeing the bear, we travelled the same distance going back in less than forty-five minutes, as I recall. I didn't think we were running, at the time, but we must have been. Actually, it was almost like flying, since I don't remember my feet touching the ground."

"I guess you had regained your full range of motion fairly quickly, then," said Victor.

"Clearly. The survival instinct kicked in and the leg muscles were fully functional again. We kept thinking the bear might change its mind and come after us, so we really applied ourselves. We probably broke the speed record for that trail — too bad nobody keeps track of such things. But there was still one more challenge waiting for us. At the end of that hike, near the mountain hut, this huge, bad-tempered dog charged towards us. We had seen it the day before, and it seemed to enjoy charging at tourists — it was a mean, surly creature, we had done our best to avoid the first time we had seen it. In any case, normally we would have been intimidated by this hound from hell, of course, but now, after coming face to face with a big bear, the mutt seemed insignificant in comparison, and we needed a release from all that tension. So, as the dog charged, instead of backing away, Gabriel and I took our hunting knives out, simultaneously, gave a triumphant battle cry — more of a primal scream, really — and charged towards the dog, as well. We obviously weren't thinking clearly, but our actions had the desired effect. The beast stopped in its tracks, visibly stunned — this was obviously an unexpected development — and then it quickly turned around and ran away from us, as fast as it could, showing us a fleeting glimpse of its big white fluffy tail. That brought our adrenalin back down, somewhat, to more manageable levels. A satisfying end to a scary day. It was the first time I had come face to face with a bear outside a zoo. Good old Gabriel… Those are the kinds of moments that cement friendships."

"Did you ever tell good old Gabriel about your plan to abandon him in front of the bear, by the way?" asked Victor.

"I didn't think he would care for those kinds of details. Besides, he never told me what he was thinking about during those moments, either. Some of these things are better left unsaid, perhaps, until many years later. I'm not even sure why I mentioned this now," concluded Alex.

"The mountain air may be to blame. The low oxygen content makes you light-headed, which may lead to inadvertent truth-telling," said Dan.

"Ease up on the plum brandy," advised Alex rather harshly, even though Dan only drank water with his dinner.

"That bear must have been one of those raised in captivity and then released for Il Presidente to shoot," said Victor, with barely disguised contempt. Out of deeply ingrained habit, he cautiously looked behind him, to check if any intruders were listening in, before continuing. "He didn't get the world record for the biggest bear ever shot for nothing, you know. You couldn't have missed that bit of news. It made the headlines several times. I heard they actually kept a secret bear farm in a remote place, near the mountains you went to that summer. To make sure the bears got really big, they fed them a lot of top-quality meat, a lot more than we ever saw in the grocery stores, and vitamins, and all the rest. Mind you, they weren't doing this out of concern for the preservation of the bears, of course. Il Presidente likes to think of himself as a peerless hunter. A hunter among hunters, you know the routine."

"I heard about that too," said Alex, intrigued. "Apparently, to keep the old man entertained, his loyal servants, the court jesters, came up with the idea of a special bear farm or enclosure, or something like that. They even had some sort of bear dietician working there. He may have been the only guy on the staff who was not a full-time member of the secret police. The only guy who didn't go to bed while wearing the telltale leather jacket, that is. Every year, these naughty, sharply dressed boys would release the biggest bears right into the middle of the forest."

"Right," Victor went on, warming up. "They would train the largest bears to come to this baited, open wooden shelter for a month or two, or maybe even longer. They would put horse meat there at regular intervals and lure bears to the area. Then, one day, the president's official helicopter would land nearby, and the old man would come near the shelter, armed to the teeth and surrounded by the equally well-armed members of his large entourage. The bear would be waiting, trapped inside the shelter and, from what I heard, usually heavily tranquilized. After the shooting was done, they all congratulated our fearless leader for the new record, and life went on, from one record year to the next. Of course, they didn't worry much about the impact of releasing too many huge farm-raised bears, with no fear of humans, in the middle of an area frequented by many hikers. No warnings were posted anywhere. Let the resourceful population fend for itself. That's probably why that big bear came right towards you on the trail. Your legendary good fortune came to your rescue once again."

"Yeah, I didn't think about it, but maybe you're right — perhaps our bear had just eaten another hiker, possibly a plump one, shortly before running into us. So, when he saw us, he probably thought: 'Man, not humans, again. I think I'll just have some berries for dessert and wash them down with creek water.' A lucky break, indeed!" said Alex.

"These rumors have been around for years. And they get more detailed and fanciful all the time. I tend to believe many of them; I really do. The story about the bear hunt seems plausible enough, given what we know, but I'm not too sure about the bear farm part. A full-time dietician? Come on! We don't even have dieticians in our hospitals, for Pete's sake. Veterinarians usually look after pets and livestock, and bears are neither. I mean, don't get me wrong guys, I like believing these sorts of things, they're good for the soul, but, ultimately, who knows?" Dan wondered aloud, hesitantly, without deliberately trying to diminish Victor's story.

"And to think that all this time I thought you were one of us," joked Victor.

But Alex looked at Dan and frowned. "Rumors are the only news that have at least a chance of being true in this surreal land of ours. Without rumors we would be completely cut off. We can't exactly conduct any independent research on these kinds of topics, can we? Can anyone imagine going to a local cop and asking, 'Excuse me, would you kindly direct me to the local bear farm, please? I'd like to see the Big Boss' next victim.'? You'd get a one-way ticket to the funny farm, or worse. In fact, we have to come all the way up here to be sure we can even talk freely about such delicate matters. Besides, we do know about the 'world record' part. I saw the winning bear hide for myself. It was indecently stretched out, behind protective glass, at the National Exhibition pavilion right beside the cultural exports section. We never used to see bears that big in our forests before. This isn't Kodiak Island, you know. And I find it very hard to believe that the old man would wander around in the forests by himself looking for gigantic, steroid-filled, carnivorous bears. Leaving aside the bear farm rumor, it's obvious the entire hunt is staged for his benefit. If the Great Man as much as sneezes, a thousand leather jackets would instantly leap to help him blow his nose. Filthy lackeys... It's hard to call that kind of execution-style shooting a sport, anyway. If you ask me, if a hunter feels brave enough and wants to get in touch with his primitive side, he should go into the forest looking for bears at night, armed only with a penknife. Now, that would be a real challenge!" Having unburdened himself of most of his temporary annoyance, Alex paused and looked straight into the fire. The fresh mountain air alone could not be counted upon to dissipate all tensions all the time.

"The only time I saw a bear in the wild, it was, fortunately, from a respectable distance away. I was on a rocky ledge, trying to photograph a small group of chamois, and, upon looking down, I saw the bear in a clearing, well below the ledge, apparently feasting among the abundant raspberry bushes," added Dan, bringing the discussion back to a more neutral ground, and feeling that he had to contribute further, even in a small way, to the conversation.

But Alex, still holding a grudge (he perceived even the slightest doubts about the truly evil nature of the entire regime as high treason), was unforgiving in his assessment of Dan's contribution: "That's it? That's your best bear story? Once upon a time, before starting med school, you used to have more of an imagination."

"It's not my fault I didn't have the good fortune of running right into a bear, like you did. I've got nothing to embellish. I did my part. I brought the tent and the better food. You can bring your stories."

"All right then. Here comes another one. And this one has all the blood and gore you seem to crave," said Alex, temporarily burying the hatchet. "Throughout my childhood, my parents believed in well balanced vacations. They were very judicious in that way. So, every summer we spent about two weeks at the seaside, which I didn't like, because it was always hot, dusty, and crowded, and two weeks in a nice small mountain resort, which was none of those things. In that small town, near the mountains, they kept a little alpine zoo I mentioned before. Bears were the main attraction. There were about six or seven of them, each in a separate enclosure. The names and birth dates of each bear were engraved on these large metal plates hung high on the bars, and the animals seemed to have fairly distinctive personalities, so I got to know them pretty well over the years. The old keeper liked me, so he let me feed the bears, once in a while. I used to bring them bread and apples, and they would all just stand there, behind the fence, with their mouths wide open, patiently waiting for me to start tossing the food over. All but Sebastian, a fairly young but very large bear, whose birthday was the same as mine. He was my favorite, so I would always give him the most apples. He never begged for food. He would simply shake the fence, each time he wanted more. He was quite aggressive sometimes, and got easily frustrated when the food I threw towards him didn't land in a convenient spot, but I always had the probably misguided feeling he would never harm me — what do you expect, I was a kid... Anyway, one summer, I came back to the zoo, and found that neither Sebastian, nor the old keeper were there any longer."

"What happened? Did the old guy let the bear go?" asked Dan.

"No such happy ending this time, I'm afraid. Didn't I just say the story was gruesome? Pay attention, damn it! The people at the zoo wouldn't answer my questions, but some local kids I knew told me the gentle old keeper had retired earlier that year. As long as he was around, there were never any problems. He was replaced by a big, sadistic young man who enjoyed poking the bears with a broom stick through the metal bars, and starving them once in a while just for kicks. What do you expect? He was the son of the local chief of police. One night, the young man got pretty drunk — not an unusual state for him — and went over to taunt Sebastian, in the usual cruel ways."

"What happened next?"

"No other people were there to witness the precise sequence of events, but the next day they found the bear sitting in his enclosure over the dismembered body of the policeman's son. The young keeper's right arm was detached from his body and tossed over to a distant corner. The broom stick was still firmly in the grip of that big right hand."

"Did they...?"

"Yes, they shot the bear, in the morning. They always shoot the bear in such cases. They say they have no choice, and all that nonsense. Too bad, really, but at least Sebastian never allowed himself to become tamed and submissive like the other bears at the zoo. He never begged for food and he took out his tormentor before dying."

"And, therefore, he saved the other bears from that sadistic keeper, as well," added Victor, with unusual emphasis.

"Right you are, Vittorio. Even bears have their heroes," said Alex, clearly pleased with Victor's observation.

"Now that you set the mood — the severed arm still holding the stick was a nice touch — do you have any other bear horror stories?" asked Victor.

"Indeed, I do. But are you sure you want to hear them, here and now?"

"Why not? I don't think I can sleep anyway, after the last one," answered Victor.

"Okay. One more then. Just so you won't be able to close your eyes in the mountains ever again. I heard it from Gabriel, a few years ago," Alex reminisced. "You may remember that strange, spooky wooded foothill called the Hunch-back..."

"Of course. The locals said there were some big bears living on that hill. That's why we always avoided it. The forest was particularly thick and dark over there — the place gave me the creeps. Even from the nearby road, you could see there was almost no space between those odd twisted and tangled trees. You couldn't help wondering what might be lurking in there," said Victor.

"That's right. I always found it rather sinister, as well. Maybe I was influenced by its name or by the locals' hostile attitude towards it. They may be ridiculously superstitious, incredibly ignorant, and disturbingly primitive, but that doesn't mean they're always wrong. Besides, there was not much there, aside from the dense woods and perhaps an old, abandoned shepherd's hut and some ancient ruins. No spectacular lookout points, no waterfalls, no great rock walls to climb — nothing for us. And it is indeed very dark in there, even during the daytime. We are diurnal creatures, for the most part, and darkness tends to make us distinctly uncomfortable. Probably why most horror stories unfold in the shadows… In any case, apparently several years ago, this hotheaded young shepherd was drinking in the main pub, in the town near this hill. After many drinks, he must have felt pretty sure of himself, because he made a bet with the bartender. The shepherd offered to leave the pub that night and hike to the top of the Hunchback Hill in the dark, before spending the night up there. In return, the bartender offered free drinks for the entire year," Alex continued.

"How would they know if the shepherd actually made it to the top of the hill during the night?" asked Dan.

"Well, apparently, on top of Hunchback Hill sat the medieval ruins of an old royal hunting lodge. I never knew about this, and you can't see any of the ruins from the town. There may just be a couple of old foundation stones left, and the crumbling remains of a wall — all well covered by many big trees, of course. Nature takes over, when we leave it alone. Anyway, the shepherd was supposed to return to the pub, as the sun rose early the next morning, carrying an artifact from the old ruin, perhaps one of the special bricks marked with the old royal emblem, or something like that. Gabriel was a bit fuzzy on the details there. Or maybe I just forgot."

This time, it was Victor's turn to ask: "How did Gabriel know about this, anyway?"

"I think he got to know the bartender, during one of his trips. You know Gabriel. He knew every bartender in every pub of every town he ever passed through. In any case, this is supposed to be a bear story, remember?" Alex reminded them. "So, the shepherd went into the night, and never came back. They waited for him at the pub, well past the time of the sunrise, the next day. Finally, in the afternoon, they organized a search party made up of fifteen or maybe twenty men, and they went looking for him." Alex paused, sipped his tea, and added another small log to the fire.

"Well, did they find him?"

"Oh, they found him, all right. What was left of him, anyway. They didn't even have to search for too long. They found his partially eaten remains scattered around, about halfway up the hill. The old watch attached to the wrist was still working — must have been a Swiss timepiece, but the wrist was no longer attached to the rest of the arm. I guess the bartender won that bet... Must have been pretty confident he would win — I mean, come on, free drinks for an entire year?"

"How did they know a bear did it?"

"Well, they had no reason to suspect the butler, did they?" said Alex. "They found bear claw marks and bite marks on the shepherd's body and bear tracks all over the place. Although I very much doubt a proper forensic investigation took place."

"You said the shepherd was drunk when he left the pub. Maybe he fell and hit his head, and then a bear came around later on. Or perhaps he upset the local chapter of the secret police," added Dan, showcasing some alternative hypotheses.

"I guess we'll never know. Perhaps the bartender's cousins did it and then framed the bear, or maybe the whole thing is just another one of Gabriel's tall pub tales. He picked up all kinds of stories during his travels. Mostly sad ones, as far as I remember. In any case, it's getting awfully late, and we have a long day ahead of us. If all goes well, by noon tomorrow, we should be able to reach the Bears' Cave," concluded Alex.

These stories were always especially poignant in the middle of this wilderness, at night. Victor closed his tired eyes and tried to imagine how many bears were silently moving through the surrounding forests at that very moment.

10

Some months perhaps adding up to more than a year or so in jail followed the inkwell incident. Gabriel couldn't remember the exact length of his sentence since, following his first encounter with the fists and the boots of the border guards, he had begun to have serious memory lapses. He also could not remember any trial preceding his sentence. A sweaty lawyer, presumably his own, had visited him briefly in prison, once. The defense lawyer, if that's who he was (Gabriel could no longer be sure), spent most of the short visit berating Gabriel and calling him a disgrace to the motherland. The broken jaw was healing slowly, but, for the entire period spent in prison, Gabriel could no longer utter a single word.

11

Bears' Cave was one of the best-kept secrets of these remote mountains. It had been discovered and explored for the first time by a team of speleologists from the National Institute only about thirty years earlier, and its whereabouts had never been widely advertised. The cave owed its name to the impressive ancient cave bear skeletons found within it. Most of these bones had been taken to the Natural History Museum in the capital, long ago. Alex's grandfather used to be a well-known professor of biology, who had worked at the museum early in his academic career. Of course, this had been before it was decided that he would be much more useful to society working as a laborer, instead. After all, what could be more important than contributing directly to the building of the canal linking the nation's largest river to the sea? At least Alex's grandfather had been fortunate to return from the canal with his health almost intact, and that in itself was quite remarkable. Many other political prisoners had not been as lucky.

Alex often visited the Natural History Museum as a child — it was one of his favorite places — and he even had occasional access to the restricted areas containing the vast research collections, which were filled with specimens the public never got to see. These collections were normally only for the use of the curators, lab technicians, and visiting researchers, but Alex was allowed in because of the respect former colleagues still had for his grandfather.

He learned early on that cave bears (*Ursus spelaeus*) belonged to a different species than the brown bears (*Ursus arctos*) which still roamed the mountain forests, and he could tell the different bear species apart simply by analyzing various features of their skeletons. While looking at some of the cave bear skulls and other huge bones in the specimen preparation labs, Alex wondered how ancient humans managed to compete for access to vital cave shelters with the mighty cave bears thousands of years ago. There must have been plenty of terrifying encounters and a lot of blood spilled. But in the end, the people obviously won and were still around in ever-increasing numbers, whereas the cave bears were gone, just like the mammoths, the woolly rhinos, and many other gigantic animals possibly hunted to extinction.

They crawled into the cave through a long, narrow tunnel, while carefully trying to avoid most of the numerous big black-and-white spiders which seemed to be taking refuge there. The tunnel, very narrow at first, became progressively wider until it opened into a stunning huge chamber in the interior of the cave. This chamber, with its thick, column-like stalagmites rising from the watery floor, resembled the interior of an enormous gothic cathedral. A flooded natural place of worship. Dark, mysterious, and vaguely intimidating. Smaller, light-pink stalactites, reflected in the waters below, emerged from among the folded bodies of thousands of bats, which covered the ceiling of the cave like a thick, soft, dark-brown blanket. The bats could enter and leave the cave through small circular openings high above, which also allowed a bit of natural light into the vast chamber. Alex remembered a story his grandfather had told him about a fellow biologist — an American — who picked up a deadly fungus while studying bats in a Jamaican cave. The fungus was new to science, and was first identified only after it was extracted from the lungs of the dead biologist.

A shallow but wide underground stream — a sheet of glistening silver cool water — was flowing over the entire floor of this portion of the cave. They started walking against the flow of the stream, hopping from rock to rock, and trying, without much success, not to get exceedingly wet.

By chance, the light beam from Alex's flashlight lingered on a peculiar small detail of the enormous cave wall, allowing him a sudden glimpse of what looked very much like a life-size carving of a bearded man's head. Briefly revealed in the flickering light, the fearless sculpted features emerged hauntingly from the surrounding rock and the almost total darkness. Intrigued, Alex approached to take a closer look. As he came near, he explored the wall, methodically, with his flashlight, for quite some time. But his thorough search failed to rediscover anything even remotely similar to the mysterious apparition. And yet, Alex felt sure that his initial observation had been correct, despite its brevity. It seemed to Alex that the carving he had seen was meant to represent the head of an ancient Dacian warrior, hidden from the prying eyes of all invaders, in a secret, sacred place.

For a moment, he wanted to alert the others and share his startling discovery with them. But the more he thought about it, the more he realized that such an action would not be advisable. Due to the poor visibility, they would most likely prove unable to locate the precise spot again, on the vast cave wall. And even if, by sheer luck, they could find the carving once again, they would probably disagree about its origin and meaning. The others wouldn't necessarily understand that ancient limestone carvings could become eroded quite a bit in this type of perpetually moist air. Victor, and especially Dan, could mistake the brave warrior's head for one of the many unusual natural formations found throughout the cave. They had little imagination — could not see past the obvious, sometimes, and their doubts would cast an undeserved shadow over the beautiful surprise of the initial discovery. Thus, Alex decided to keep his precious find to himself, and not waste any more time second guessing the validity of his impressions. Furthermore, they were already running a bit late, and he couldn't remember exactly how long the half-walk, half-crawl through the corridor was supposed to take. Victor was moving steadily ahead, oblivious to Alex's lucky find, and Dan seemed to be lagging hopelessly behind, for some unknown reason. If we lose him, we'll also lose the tent and the chocolates, Alex said to himself.

The air became considerably colder as they walked deeper into the cave. There were no more bats above their heads, and even with the flashlights on, it was becoming harder to penetrate the all-encompassing darkness. The wet walls were scarred by the openings of many mysterious secondary tunnels, which, for the most part, were much too narrow and inaccessible to explore. Even though this did not seem either logical or likely, the unsettling shifting shadows all around encouraged the young explorers to imagine that some undiscovered monsters, endemic to the cave, could somehow leap out of the tunnels and take them away at any moment.

"I don't remember the water being this deep before," said Victor, who was already in water up to his thighs. "I wonder how much deeper it's going to get. You know I don't swim well."

"Don't worry pal, I'm right behind you. The moment you disappear below the water, I promise to stop advancing and turn around to get some help," replied Alex, with his proven talent for calming everybody down in tough moments.

"Well, one quick downpour outside, and we'll probably all drown in here, like rats," added Victor, and this new imagined danger made him pick up the pace.

"Look on the bright side," came Alex's powerful voice, booming as it became amplified in the hollow chamber. "In a few hundred years, they might find our bones, and put us in a museum. They'll probably label us as ancient warriors."

"Or just dumb tourists," mumbled Victor, looking frantically for a way out of the underground maze.

Dan was still trailing far behind the others, having scraped his knee quite badly in the dark against the sharp edge of a protruding rock, which could very well have been an overlooked fossilized cave bear skull.

Fortunately, they soon reached the point where the stream emerged from behind the lower edge of a slippery limestone wall. Relief flooded over them, for they remembered that place, and they also remembered to look along that wall for the small tunnel which would take them away from the stream and towards another exit of the cave. They crawled along the tunnel for a long time, occasionally having to wiggle mightily in order to squeeze through a few of the tighter spots.

"It seemed so much easier the last time," said Alex, slightly wheezing. "I refuse to believe I've put on that much weight since then! You have to be a bloody mole, or an earthworm, to get through here."

Finally, they emerged out of the cold cave and into the welcoming warm rays of the afternoon sun.

12

They sat in the pleasant meadow outside the second entrance into the cave, and allowed themselves to dry out in the gentle sun. After the considerable efforts required to get through the Bears' Cave with their backpacks, they decided, unanimously, to set camp in the meadow until the next morning.

"I wonder where that stream comes from?" asked Dan, eager to show his more adventurous side, after having failed so miserably the night before in the bear story category, and prominently displaying the fresh cut on his knee as a badge of honor. "It might be interesting to dive below the limestone wall, and try to reemerge on the other side, in order to follow the stream to its real source."

"You cannot be serious! There may not be another side for miles. And even if you could actually squeeze under the lower edge of that wall, which I doubt, who knows when, or if, you would be able to come up for air again, after you dove down there," answered Victor, trying to nip any attempt at reentering the cave in the bud.

"I was simply saying it could be interesting to discover the source. That's all," said Dan, a bit defensively.

"Yeah, it could also be interesting to take a flying leap from the top of that big cliff in the distance. I think I can live without knowing exactly where the damn stream I almost drowned in comes from," added Alex in his typically diplomatic way.

"I'm with Alex on this one. In any case, I'm certainly not the man for the job, since, as I said, I don't swim well. And let's not forget the risk of hypothermia — I've been shivering for half an hour. I'll wait for you here, if you're crazy enough to try it! I guess I should warn you though that if you're not back by dinnertime, Alex and I will be glad to share your food ration, as well," said Victor.

"Absolutely!" agreed Alex, readily. "Hiking in the mountains can be tough, and there's no room for the faint of heart up here. Some make it, and some don't. It's just the way it is. So, if you get stuck on the other side of that wall, I want you to know we won't let your Swiss chocolates and all your other fancy food supplies go to waste. We'll enjoy them, like I know you would want us to, old pal. Your generosity won't be forgotten. We may even have a toast in your honor. Or not. And, by the way, if the unthinkable happens and you don't return, could I have your flexible fiberglass tent poles? I promise to take very good care of them."

"All right, all right, you talked me out of it! I was merely curious, anyway," laughed Dan. "I didn't realize before just how persuasive the two of you can be when you team up against someone. It's just too bad you've lost some of your thirst for exploring the unknown. Luckily, I'm here to keep the standards high in that respect."

"What you call 'thirst for exploring the unknown' sounds like a suicide attempt to me," said Victor, immediately regretting his words.

"Let's ease up on that kind of talk," mentioned an unusually subdued Alex, and they all fell silent, remembering the main purpose of their journey.

The small meadow, surrounded by fairly steep cliffs, provided them with an ideal, sheltered camping site. Just enough wind came through the small spaces between the wide cliffs to provide a pleasant cool breeze. A few long-dead dwarf pines, found near the cave entrance, were a good source of reasonably dry wood for the fire, and a small creek brought fresh water from a nearby glacier. All the key ingredients were in place for a worry-free evening. Alex started the fire, his favorite task, and Dan struggled to fill the large metal pot, which had been almost completely blackened by the flames of many fires over the years, with relatively clean water from the creek, while simultaneously trying to keep small pebbles and sand out.

"Don't be too fussy about the water," Alex loved to say. "There's probably always a mountain goat, or a deer, peeing upstream, anyway."

After three days, dinner preparations now also involved the careful separation of the remaining edible food supplies from the no longer edible, and potentially dangerous, ones. Questions such as: "Are these raisins or bat droppings?", "How did this cheese become the greenest thing in your backpack?", "Do you think we can at least use this bit of salami as an insect repellent?" and a few other, more probing, ones were certainly asked during this vital selection process. The savage downpour from two nights ago had left many of their food supplies quite wet, and the pervasive wetness speeded up the inevitable decomposition process.

"Just boil the hell out of everything," advised Alex.

Fortunately, the food only served as the preamble to the coffee, and the coffee was still good. Dan was the only one who did not have an additional cup.

"I always get an uncontrollable surge of energy after more than one cup of coffee, and my pulse goes up quite a bit. And it's already high enough as it is. I'd be climbing those cliffs all night," he explained.

"Maybe you should have an extra cup tomorrow morning. You looked kind of sluggish in the cave today. For a while, I thought you were actually going to pass out and drown right in the middle of that underground stream," said Alex, winking.

Dan ignored the mild ribbing and continued: "My former girlfriend used to be able to drink eight cups a day. I never understood how she could do it. Coffee never seemed to affect her at all. Maybe she just became immune to the effects, over time. We would have run out of coffee after the first day, if she would have come with us on this trip."

"I don't think there would have been any danger of that," said Alex.

"Why? We don't actually have that much coffee — it isn't that easy to get these days, you know," Dan replied, a bit puzzled.

"No, I meant there was no realistic chance she would be coming," Alex explained.

"Actually, you may laugh, but, for a few days, I toyed with the idea of asking her to come along — just as a friend, of course. A sort of final reunion for all of us. I thought that might be nice. She always loved the mountains, as you know. But I wasn't sure how she would take it, all things considered, and I also didn't know how you would react. Plus, we would have needed an extra tent. In the final analysis, it was easier not to ask," Dan confessed.

"How is she, these days? Do you know?" asked Alex.

"Not really. We don't keep in touch. I don't think she's dating anyone, from what I hear, but I don't really know. I see her occasionally at the university, walking down the corridor between classes, but we're not in the same study groups. It's awkward. I never know what to say when I see her, so I end up sounding like an idiot. Fortunately, it no longer matters that much," said Dan.

"Cheer up! A few more years and you'll both graduate, and you won't have to worry about seeing her or finding the right words," said Alex.

"Yeah, sure. That's great, but graduation is still a long way away. Plenty of time for more humiliations. Do you want me to give her a message?" asked Dan.

Alex didn't answer him directly. Instead, he said: "Among all of my many acquaintances, the two of you used to be my one and only example of a nice and seemingly well-adjusted young couple. A tad too nice and a bit too well-adjusted for my taste, if you must know. And both aspiring doctors, no less... You seemed trapped in a harmonious relationship, if only for a little while. I found it quite unsettling, actually, and I couldn't really understand it. So, come clean with us, why did you and Dana split up, anyway? What's the real story behind all the sordid rumors I started about you two?"

"We just couldn't cope with the concept of the matching first names, I suppose," said Dan, a bit stung by what he perceived as Alex's sarcasm. It felt like applying pressure to sunburned skin.

"Yes, that is always a relationship killer, I know. I would never date anyone named Alexandra, for example. It would make introductions much too awkward," said Alex, trying to keep the discussion light-hearted.

"Sometimes, the pieces of the puzzle just don't fit together properly," said Dan, who was now suddenly in a somber mood.

"I'm sorry, but that is much too cryptic, and I am too tired now to analyze all the possible interpretations," said Alex, faking a yawn. He did not expect an additional explanation from Dan.

But Dan felt he had to add a few more generalities and explain himself further. Otherwise, the others might have been left with the mistaken impression that he was still hung up on Dana. He somehow had to come up with a more coherent and neutral version of events.

"Well, if you must know, we got together with great expectations, I think — well, okay, maybe that's not quite true. I don't know about her, but at least I had high hopes at first, and then we spent the next year or so watching all those expectations dwindle and fade, one by one, until there was nothing left but to say good-bye. In the end, there was not even enough passion for any hard feelings. We didn't even argue. The whole relationship simply fizzled out, like stale champagne. I am still not quite sure why things turned out the way they did. I can guess, but I can never be sure. She's beautiful, as you know, but she never seemed really happy. She always gave me the feeling that something was missing, and there was nothing I could do about it." For a brief moment, he was unable to hide his disappointment in its entirety. And then he stopped, suddenly aware that he had already said much more than he really wanted to. Especially to Alex.

"That was straightforward. Straight out of the brochure. In any case, watching the two of you part ways shattered my last illusion of the potentially perfect couple. That's when I decided I should stick to what I know best: brief, meaningless affairs," said Alex, with a bit of a forced smile, feeling somewhat guilty about his previous direct questions which led to Dan's unexpected and uncomfortable confession. Attempting to quickly change the subject, Alex continued: "Of course, there are also more responsible citizens among us. Take old Vic, here, for example!"

Victor, quietly pleased to have been left out of the conversation until that moment, replied defensively, "It's true, up to a point. Yes, I should actually marry Silvia, in due course, but nothing has been decided yet. No date has been set. She'll have to get her teaching certificate first, and I'll have to see about trying to postpone military service for another year. I don't know if that will be possible again. I'm sort of running out of convincing medical excuses. The more I try to look ill, the better I feel."

"Staying out of the army has that kind of positive effect on one's health. Look at me, for instance — I'm embarrassingly healthy, knock on wood. Never did a second of government-mandated service of any kind, and I'm damn proud of it," said Alex.

"Yeah, but eventually, even those dim sergeants at the recruitment office will slowly figure out that some of my numerous excuses may not be entirely legitimate," Victor continued.

"Don't overestimate them," Alex helpfully intervened. "Those loathsome morons barely have enough brain capacity for the partial control of basic bodily functions and the torture of new recruits."

"In another few years, perhaps Dan will be able to write all the medical notes I'll ever need," Victor added, almost wistfully.

"That's only if he gets over his broken heart, stops wasting time hanging around with anti-social elements like us, and really applies himself to his studies. They don't just give those medical degrees away from the back of a truck, you know. At least, not yet. Besides, he doesn't have enough money or cigarettes to bribe all his professors, or enough political connections to impress anyone that matters," warned Alex.

"In the meantime, however, I'll have to try even harder than before to fake an illness or two, despite my limited acting abilities," concluded Victor, focusing solely on the big task that awaited him.

"What are you worried about? You're practically blind, you have high blood pressure, you were wheezing on the mountain as if you had worked for twenty years in a local coal mine, and there's probably only a tiny bit of blood left in all that cholesterol clogging your thickened veins. You have everything you need," said Alex, trying to sound reassuring.

"Thanks, but that may still not be enough. Besides, there is also the timing of the upcoming wedding to consider. I don't know, there's a lot to think about... Too much, perhaps."

"You better marry her if you want to avoid military service. Isn't her father a big shot colonel of some sort? If you don't marry her, he'll probably pay very special attention to you, and you'll find yourself doing two years of hard time, patrolling the western border!" said Alex, cheerfully. He could imagine Victor innocently adjusting his thick glasses, while walking near the imposing electrified barbed wire fence and holding an overeager German shepherd on a tight leash.

Victor was not inclined to take such a frightening prospect lightly, however: "They wouldn't put a young engineer on the border patrol. As you helpfully pointed out, I can barely see two meters in front of me, on a good day. They need their special soldiers there. The ones who wouldn't hesitate to shoot defectors on sight. And go for the head or the chest, not just the legs. Of course, it's easy for you to joke about these things. You no longer have to worry about the army or anything else, since you'll be flying over that damned border soon!" There was a brief pause, and they subsequently found it hard to look at one another.

Alex, as usual, was the first who felt the need to break the suddenly oppressive silence: "That's true enough now, although the bastards could still try to trip me up until the very last minute — I wouldn't put it past them. But I did have many good reasons to worry before. I waited for the approval to come for almost two years — you know that. During that entire period, I was waiting in purgatory, and they could have drafted me at any time, or worse. They threatened me with everything under the sun. The army, hard labor, and all sorts of other such things. They called me a vagrant, and they called my parents traitors. All of a sudden, I no longer had a clear status within this society. I was no longer an anonymous student hidden in the crowd. I became someone whose background was being actively looked into, and whose future was being assessed at higher levels. Strange people in long overcoats started to come around in order to ask my neighbors about me. Some old acquaintances started avoiding me, after they had found out. It's as if I had suddenly developed plague symptoms, as far as they were concerned. I could see that their cowardice made them uneasy, when we met accidentally, but they couldn't help trying to protect their own interests. In a way, I could understand them. After all, unlike me, they had to stay behind and face the future here. But still, it was hard to forgive — there are too many damn cowards and informers crawling and lurking around here. And I'm not the forgiving kind, anyway. That was a good time to find out about true friends. Now that the matter seems to be finally settled, or almost settled, I'm sort of looking forward to experiencing my first Canadian winter soon. That may be something else to worry about, mes braves amis!"

"You know I envy you a bit, but, if I can't get out of this place, I'm at least happy that you can. Make us proud over there. Maybe one day I'll also get to see the other side for myself. I always wanted to see Paris, at least once, and Vienna, and Venice, and so many other places… Perhaps we'll go hiking in the Alps or the Rockies someday, before we get too old and decrepit. Who knows? In any case, with you about to go overseas for good, and Victor looking to get married, this is truly the end of an era, my friends," said Dan, magnanimously raising his empty cup.

"The end of life as we know it," added Alex, lifting his cup as well to meet Dan's.

"Certainly, the end of life as you've known it," concluded Victor, looking at Alex.

13

The middle-aged truck driver was passionately sucking on the dwindling, lit butt of what had once been a full, homemade cigarette. He was leaning on a truck which looked like it must have been almost new around the time of his birth. Two large gobblers were resting nearby, beside an old, obsolete tractor tire. A banal local folk song, sang by a female with an excessively high-pitched voice, came blaring out of the vibrating small transistor radio attached with masking tape to the dashboard of the run-down truck. The song told an irritatingly moralistic little tale about a young man who had to give up booze, in order to prevent the young women of his village from making fun of him.

"Good day. I was wondering if you could be so kind as to give us a ride, at your convenience, to the old alpine shelter," Dan asked, cutting to the chase.

"I reckon I could, if we can reach some sort of understanding. Fuel is getting awfully expensive, these days, for us common people," the truck driver answered, carefully putting aside the cigarette butt to take a swig of homemade liquor, straight from a voluminous demijohn. The impressive loudness of his own ensuing burp made him beam proudly, as he generously pushed the demijohn towards his future customers.

"If any of you can top that burp of mine, I'll take you there for half-price," he added.

But the meal in the tavern had weakened the young men's resolve, and, upon looking at the imperfectly distilled liquid in the dirty demijohn, they wisely declined to accept that noble challenge. Instead, they talked briefly among themselves, under the driver's steady stare, before making the offer which led, after a bit of mild haggling, to the anticipated understanding.

"There's only room for one of you inside, on the seat beside me. The rest of you, and your backpacks, will have to go on the logs at the back," the driver explained, needlessly wiping his dirty hands on his already soiled sleeveless undershirt. A sense of solidarity forced all three young men to get up on the unstable pile of logs and take their chances.

"At least, it's easier to jump out from the back, in case this guy takes a wrong turn, and guides this wreck off some cliff," Alex whispered, and the others quietly nodded in agreement.

"Don't worry about a thing," the driver added, sensing their unease. "I'll get you there, all right. Just remember to lie low on the logs, 'cause if the cops see you, I'll have to say I don't know how you got there, and you'll be on your own. Other than that, you've got nothing to worry about. As soon as I finish my drink, we'll be on our way." He then flicked away the still burning cigarette butt, barely missing an open fuel drum, and started to whistle towards the irritable gobblers, causing them to instantly puff up and explode in a flurry of indignant calls.

14

In the morning, after looking at their maps for quite a long time, they had to agree, reluctantly, that the only feasible way of reaching Bandits' Mountain, their next major destination, was through the dreaded Valley of the Vipers. True to its name, the narrow valley, covered with unusually tall grasses, sheltered a notorious population of rare adders, whose powerful poison could kill even adult humans in only a few agonizing hours.

"I believe they have hemotoxic venom, which usually breaks down capillary walls and destroys the blood cells. Of course, there could be other complications, as well. It's really quite horrible," Dan pointed out.

"Thank you for the unsolicited explanation, doctor. If you would have remembered to bring the antivenin serum, as we had discussed, we wouldn't have quite as much to worry about now, would we?" said Victor, accusingly.

"The serum they had at the clinic wasn't all that reliable anyway. It could probably kill you just as fast as the snake bite," Dan answered, trying to divert attention from his glaring oversight.

"Well, it's too late for insincere apologies now. Let's just take our chances. Gentlemen, the viper pit is beckoning," Alex summed up. He was hoping the snakes would be more sluggish and less likely to attack in the cool morning, before their cold-blooded bodies had a chance to warm up in the afternoon heat. He also knew, although he didn't want to mention it and worry his friends, that this was the time of the year when the female adders were more likely to give birth, and this made them particularly aggressive towards potential intruders. Unfortunately, the well-camouflaged snakes were virtually invisible through the tall, thick vegetation. Therefore, the likelihood of inadvertently stepping on a sluggish adder was unsettlingly high. Alex grabbed his sturdy alpenstock, and started to clear the path ahead, through the grasses which almost matched his considerable height.

"I heard this valley had been the site of some fierce battles in the distant past. Apparently, the grasses are unusually tall here because of all the extra nutrients provided by all the corpses left to rot in these fields after the fighting," Dan heard himself mention.

"That's a great story. You should have saved it for lunch," Victor observed.

"Maybe the nutrients keep coming from the steady flow of snake bite victims," Alex concluded, swinging the staff through the thick clumps of vegetation with increasing determination.

The faint rustling sounds caused by the light wind meandering through the fairly dry grasses were eerily similar to the imagined treacherous noises of slithering snake bodies, which must have been present all around. These shadowy bastards, crawling quietly almost everywhere, sometimes ready to strike, but mostly toying with people's nerves, reminded Alex of the dreaded secret police which had infested so many of his thoughts during the last few years. If only secret policemen were as rare in this country as these adders, he thought. He remembered the telling double clicks at the end of each of his long-distance conversations with his parents. The first click would come after his parents would hang up, and the second click would be heard several seconds later, after the secret policeman, who would be always listening in, would stop his tape recorder. Sometimes, the pause between the two clicks would last a minute or more (maybe the secret policeman was taking a bathroom break), and, in those instances, Alex got into the habit of staying on the line, singing Beatles songs, until he heard the second click. He wanted to let those snooping scumbags know that he knew they were there. If they insisted on listening in, each bloody week, they might as well get to record some good music and some top-notch singing, in addition to the private conversations. Later on, it dawned on Alex that, perhaps, the "secret" policemen, with their conspicuous second clicks, wanted him to know they were always there, hovering around in the background. Perhaps they were trying to intimidate or annoy him. Maybe they foolishly thought he would lose his nerve and withdraw his application to emigrate. Or, maybe, they just didn't care. They had to do their jobs, and it didn't matter if they were heard or seen by the people they were after. They knew they would never have to be accountable to their victims.

Alex gripped the alpenstock and swung it powerfully towards the ground, impaling a hissing adder, which had adopted a typical, low striking posture.

Dan, who followed Alex closely, through the grasses, felt suddenly sick at the sight of the thick, dying snake, slowly twisting on the sharp, iron-tipped end of the spear-like alpenstock. All his careless talk of hemotoxic venom and rotting corpses ceased to be merely abstract, and Dan wondered if he were meant to die young among the tall grasses growing in this remote field. Upon seeing Dan's ghostly white face and the by-now dead adder, Victor did not show any emotion but did stop to carefully tuck his faded blue jeans into his old hiking boots. Alex threw the lifeless snake body as far away as he could and watched it disappear behind the thick curtain of vegetation. The moment the body of the snake landed in the distance, they heard a startlingly low grunt, which seemed to have originated in the larynx of a very large being.

"Vic, please tell me that sound was produced by the clearing of your throat," Alex said, slowly.

"Sorry to disappoint you Al, but I don't think that was a human sound," Victor whispered in reply.

"What do you think we're dealing with?" asked Dan, turning even whiter than before — something that had not seemed possible just a few seconds earlier.

"Wild boar or bear. Almost equally bad news in a field like this. I must have really hit the target with that stupid dead snake," said Alex.

"It was the dead snake's revenge," added Victor.

Almost immediately after Victor's brief comment, the unidentified large being started to move through the grasses in a difficult-to-determine direction. The young men walked slowly away, loudly singing an old Beatles song, *Yellow Submarine*, in order to keep their spirits up and advertise their human identity to the unknown resident whose rest they had inadvertently disturbed.

After their fifth consecutive, and loudest, rendition of the song, they emerged unscathed from the field of tall grasses, and found themselves at the edge of the valley, near the foot of a very steep mountain.

Dan collapsed to the ground and mumbled something about having to skip lunch. Victor sat quietly on a rock, took off his glasses, and started to wipe the thick lenses with a clean handkerchief he had brought along for that very purpose. The glasses with the sturdy, old-fashioned black frames represented Victor's most vital possession. At night, in the tent, he always kept them nearby, in a special small protective case, safely away from his tent mates' carelessness. He knew all too well that if anything were to happen to his glasses, he would have been virtually helpless, and almost entirely dependent on his friends for guidance on the narrow alpine trails. Victor wondered what would have become of him if he had been born before glasses were invented.

Alex was the only one still standing, near the last of the tall grasses. Since his perfect vision could not help him penetrate the thick vegetation, he was trying hard to listen for telling sounds of approaching danger. No such sounds could be heard, and Alex felt relieved, although there seemed to be a very slight odd scent in the air, which he could not quite account for. He also could not explain why that particular, barely detectable, smell made him feel strangely anxious deep inside.

"Well, what's on your mind?" asked Dan, whose general condition seemed to be rapidly improving.

"I was just thinking that you still can't carry a tune," answered Alex, cheerfully, causing Victor to smile and Dan to feel his cheeks turning slightly red, matching the natural color of his hair and his numerous freckles. Dan had never been heard to admit that his hair was actually a bright shade of reddish-orange. He had always maintained, stubbornly, that he was a true blond, and his self-conscious assertions on the subject always caused great amusement among his friends. Dan knew he shouldn't take Alex's light comments too seriously, but, sometimes, he just couldn't help feeling the sting of those friendly jabs. He thought about replying that one didn't need to be an expert at carrying a tune in order to sing an easy song such as *Yellow Submarine*. If it weren't an easy song to sing, the other Beatles wouldn't have given Ringo the opportunity of taking over as the lead vocalist. Could anyone seriously imagine Ringo sing *Yesterday*, for example? Tone-deaf football fans in stadiums all over the country, and in the rest of Europe, managed to get through that inspired, upbeat little melody without excessive trouble, while replacing the lyrics about the world-famous submarine with new ones related to their favorite teams. However, Dan realized he had unfortunately waited much too long to think of a suitable answer to Alex's initial remark. By now, the others had moved on to other topics, and his reply would certainly appear to be awkward and ill-timed. Thus, he kept the remark to himself, and did his best to catch up with the current conversation.

As they celebrated the crossing of the Valley of the Vipers with an ultra-light snack of crackers and orange juice, feeling good about themselves, the big old bear watched them patiently from his hiding place among the sheltering grasses, through his one good eye.

15

They were introduced to the music of the Beatles in the second year of high school, about eight years after the world's most celebrated rock band had ceased to exist. It happened when Gabriel brought an old, scratched copy of the *Rubber Soul* LP over, during a party at Dan's place, on the outskirts of the capital. The impact was not immediate. At the time, disco music reigned supreme, and Gabriel's record was barely played at the party. But Alex, who found most disco music as predictably boring and painfully simple-minded as the presidential speeches, was intrigued enough to ask for permission to borrow the album, for a careful, and more private, listening session.

The Beatles were just a few years younger than Alex's parents. During his childhood, Alex had occasionally heard the word "beatles." It seemed to be used derisively by some older adults to describe young men, usually university students, with long hair (who were rarely seen in those days on the grimy streets of their gray capital). Thus, as a child, he thought that any such young men were "beatles." Years later, he learned the true meaning of that strange foreign word, which couldn't be found in the English dictionary. Until the aftermath of Dan's party, however, Alex did not find out much more about the famous group the name belonged to.

On the Sunday which followed Dan's party, Alex, Victor, and Dan got together, at Alex's apartment, to make copies of the Beatles' record using Dan's East German turntable, Alex's Dutch cassette tape recorder and Victor's homemade connection cables. Victor, who had a passion for cables and electronic gadgets, was one of the very few people competent enough to complete a successful link between the Eastern turntable and the Western cassette player. During the lengthy waiting periods which accompanied the taping sessions, they looked at the cover of the record, trying to figure out which Beatle name belonged to each Beatle face.

Victor thought (correctly, as it turned out) that Ringo was the shortest one of the four, and, thus, the third one from the left on the album cover. They all thought Paul, who was still writing hit songs long after the break-up of the Beatles, was probably the one standing to the right of Ringo. After that, the guessing game reached an insurmountable impasse. Without additional information, they had no way of being sure which of the other two was John and which was George. The rather unusual cover photograph, which showed somewhat elongated versions of the band members' faces, did not help the identification process.

From that day forward, for the next couple of years, they tried to learn as much as possible about Paul's former band. Many well-worn vinyl records, poor quality tapes, and old, sometimes barely relevant newspaper clippings travelled back and forth among the three friends, until they had a fairly complete collection of Beatles songs, on tape, and a pretty good understanding of what all the fuss had been about. By the time the sad news of John's assassination in New York City travelled over borders around the world, Alex could reliably identify, in each case, which of the many Lennon-McCartney songs were John's, which were Paul's, and which belonged to both of them. He had come a long way from the day when he couldn't tell John and George apart, while looking at the front cover of *Rubber Soul*.

16

Bandits' Mountain, the highest peak in the faraway mountain chain, had remained unconquered during their previous trips to the area. This was due in part to the fact that the strange-looking crooked peak was often surrounded by dark clouds, even when all the other nearby mountains were bathing in sunlight, and partly because the climb appeared obviously difficult even in the unlikely event of good weather. But this time, as they had all agreed before the trip, they were going to make it all the way up Bandits' Mountain, regardless of weather conditions and despite the inevitable last-minute jitters. Their last trip together would have to be crowned by a special achievement, something they could all regard as important and treasure for many years to come.

They left the still-heavy backpacks resting against the foot of a nearby boulder. Going up with a substantial load was out of the question, and they thought that if everything went well, they could be back down by the late afternoon or early evening. From their current location, the climb to the top of the mountain was estimated to last about two to three hours, depending on the route chosen and the level of a climber's experience, and the descent could take almost as long. The night before, they had studied handwritten notes and rudimentary maps related to the ascent, which had been given to them by an experienced middle-aged mountaineer who had climbed all the difficult peaks in that region multiple times. The man had lost a good friend during an ill-considered early spring ascent of Bandits' Mountain, and he had advised them against trying to reach the peak.

"I'm not a superstitious man," he had said, "but there is something about that mountain. Things often seem to go wrong there."

Dan quietly distributed small glucose tablets for much-needed energy. This also provided an even more badly needed distraction from dark thoughts of sudden, possibly fatal, falls and other complications. Still, some serious doubts inevitably remained.

"Doesn't the *Blue Mountain Guidebook*, a publication I actually respect, advise that this climb should not be attempted without safety rope?" asked Victor, as he looked up at the imposing granite wall rising discouragingly perpendicular in relation to the ground under their feet. One wrong move, and this hard ground would become a final resting place.

"Not to worry, Vic. With our lack of fitness and experience, it probably doesn't matter. On this mountain, we can fail just as easily with or without the stinking rope," Alex reassured him, before pausing briefly to analyze the best way of pursuing the early phase of the inevitable upcoming ascent. Having visualized a suitable way up the mountain in his mind's eye, he added, with a mixture of relief and slight disdain: "At least we're not dealing with the North Face of the Eiger here."

"That's right," Victor replied firmly. "Here, there are no well-equipped rescue teams ready to save crazy climbers, and no cables left into the rock by previous alpinists. Nobody will find us 'till next spring."

"Well, at least we know there's absolutely no reason for a false sense of security," said Alex, as he started making his way up the wall in a determined and methodical fashion. Every crevice in his path had to be evaluated carefully for its potential in assisting or compromising the challenging climb. Some crevices were large enough for footholds, some were useful for hand, finger or even fingertip holds, while others were obviously much too small or irregular, and did not provide any assistance. It was invigorating to have to pay maximum attention to every single move.

Alex loved the solitude of climbing, and the heightened awareness which could only be induced by immediate serious risks. He felt much more comfortable climbing on his own, without a rope. Somehow, he could never get himself to accept the idea that his own life should depend on such impossible-to-control variables as the sturdiness of a piece of rope, the amount of rust in an old piton, or the judgement of a possible climbing partner he would find himself tied to. It was always better to rely solely on oneself, taking full responsibility for one's mistakes and full — and well-deserved — credit for one's triumphs. The courageous quest for difficult-to-achieve successes, despite the keen awareness of potential dangers and pitfalls, made the game of life worth playing, with utmost intensity and dedication, until the very end.

He was climbing gracefully and effortlessly, aware of his strength, concentrating on the obstacles on his path, while at the same time subconsciously reducing his anxiety by allowing himself to daydream. In school, one of his teachers had called that rare quality "distributive attention," or the ability to keep one's mind, equally well, on several matters at the same time. It wasn't clear whether the teacher's comments were meant as a compliment or an indictment. While searching for a precise definition of his condition in his grandfather's French encyclopedia, Alex had discovered, with satisfaction, that Napoleon Bonaparte had had a similar affliction.

During most lectures, Alex was known to divide his time between sharing subversive jokes with nearby fellow students and allowing his thoughts to wander far beyond the walls of the classroom. And yet, the teachers' surprise questions, designed to entrap and impeach him, never caught him unprepared. A part of his mind always remained connected, almost subconsciously, to his teachers' boring, predictable sermons, and that fragile connection allowed him the luxury of using many of the endless school hours for unadulterated daydreaming. Of course, some lectures, on subjects related to literature, philosophy, history, biology, or physics, for instance, were actually worth listening to, once in a while, whereas French and, especially, English lessons would surely prove to be most useful in the long run. Sadly, however, their overly crowded high school curriculum had also included too many other courses, such as Marxist-Leninist Social Economics (taught by a former party activist whose alcoholism masked some of the symptoms of his almost certain insanity), and lectures on the intricacies of factory work and heavy machinery (taught by a stuttering foreman, plucked straight from the factory floor, whose speech impediment couldn't always hide his total lack of familiarity with basic grammar).

Alex thought a more suitable title for the Marxist-Leninist Social Economics course would have been: "How to Ruin The Economy, and Society in General, and Then Lie About It." He figured out very early that the course was not based on any known economic principles. The teacher made up his own rules, and the answer to any problem or question was always, "The communist system is superior." When it came to such courses, the only tough part was taking them seriously. If you could learn to regurgitate the ideological drivel with a straight face, you were all set.

Alex's good grades in all courses (even Marxist-Leninist Social Economics) were a grudging tribute by his teachers, but predictably, his biting sarcasm was utterly unappreciated by most of his educators, whose stiffness Alex could only explain as the inevitable result of broom sticks inserted far up the rectum. His reputation for causing mischief was such that whenever any student nearby would laugh, smile, or smirk, for whatever reason, Alex would automatically get blamed.

The occasion of Mao's death was a perfect example. As fellow communist dictators, the rulers of their land decided Mao's passing had to be suitably honored. And so it was that Mao's death, in faraway China, was officially declared a reasonable cause for a national day of mourning in their small European country. On that day, Alex's class, together with other groups of students and workers, had the good fortune of being chosen to bring the nation's "spontaneous" expressions of grief to the attention of the officials at the Chinese embassy, in the capital. This turned out to be an incredibly tough assignment for a group of very active youngsters in grade eight, who were actually thrilled to get an unexpected day off from school. Needless to say, none of them were particularly upset about Mao's passing, which seemed like an abstract notion, and the pressure of having to act solemn and sad, while presenting "most sincere" condolences in front of the seemingly devastated Chinese officials and the stern-looking representatives of their own government, led to barely controllable attacks of hysterical laughter among the weaker students. Even the accompanying teacher, to her obvious horror, had caught the powerful and extremely contagious laughter germ from her students. Luckily, all those muffled whimpering sounds could be mistaken for signs of extreme sadness by inattentive listeners. As a general rule, if you want to cause a bunch of healthy kids to lose all composure in mere minutes, all you have to do is tell them they are not allowed to laugh under any circumstances, and then watch them closely.

The Chinese embassy was located in a big, intimidating building. The students had to cross the wide hall on the first floor of the embassy and shake hands with several officials, before dutifully signing their names in a huge book of condolences. Alex had been taught that shaking hands vigorously was a sign of respect, so he really applied himself, and shook the officials' hands as strongly as he could. He was surprised that their grips were comparatively weak, but thought they may have been tired after shaking hundreds, or perhaps even thousands, of hands that day. The Chinese officials looked quite pale and close to fainting from grief. Alex wondered if the officials were all truly as sad as they appeared or if they feared the consequences of not looking distressed enough in front of their colleagues and bosses.

Alex, whose well-developed will power allowed him to suppress his laughter, did not like the idea of being coerced into attaching his name to what he perceived as official embassy documents. Who could tell where such documents would be stored, or who would check these names one day? What if he would make something of himself, and then someone would come out and say: "Look, he wrote his name in there. Perhaps this reflects his early political views."

Since there didn't seem to be any way of avoiding the unpleasant task, Alex had the presence of mind of solving his dilemma by signing a name other than his own in the book of condolences. Unfortunately, the name he came up with, on the spur of the moment, was Napoleon Bonaparte. His teacher, who was next in line and had the misfortune of noticing Alex's signature, promptly burst out laughing. The high-pitched, wild laughter cascaded unexpectedly, almost painfully, from the teacher's throat, filling the large chamber of the embassy and causing instant panic among the formerly somber officials.

In the end, the embassy visit turned into a scandalous international incident. As a result, in the principal's office the next day, Alex, who hadn't laughed, got blamed not only for his controversial signature but also for the teacher's obvious lack of self-control. Only his good grades, his young age, and the teacher's surprisingly passionate intervention on his behalf saved Alex from a lengthy suspension.

The teacher, however, was not as lucky. Her suspension was much longer, and both the location and the exact nature of her next assignment remained unknown.

Alex's flow of reminiscences, as well as his steady climbing, were rudely interrupted by a terrifying bolt of lightning, which crashed unexpectedly into a mountain wall nearby with tremendous force, rattling nerves and rock formations alike. It felt like a mini-earthquake, as if the mountains were coming alive and dancing in place. The three friends were getting close to the summit — closer than they had ever been before — but now they all stopped at the same time, trying to come to terms with the worsening weather. Alex suddenly remembered, from an obscure seventh grade geography lesson, that these mountains sheltered substantial iron ore deposits. Storm clouds were quickly gathering around the peak, hiding it from sight. Looking up became much harder for the climbers since they were hit by a troublesome burst of pea-sized hail. Their situation changed from somewhat difficult to very dangerous in mere seconds.

Alex regained his composure and hauled himself onto a narrow ledge, which led to a providential cozy grotto carved into the side of the mountain. He then turned around, leaned over, and extended a welcome helping hand to Victor, who was close behind and advancing along the wall in a typically workmanlike fashion. As they took refuge in the grotto, they waited for Dan to join them. Almost ten minutes passed, however, and Dan did not appear. Alex and Victor could see him from the ledge. He seemed glued to the wall, not too far down, frozen by the rapidly unfolding storm and incapable of advancing towards relative safety. The now pouring rain was making the rocks slippery, and Dan's situation was becoming more and more precarious by the minute.

Alex, knowing he had to intervene, called out, "Danny, listen to me. This is not the time to discover your latent acrophobia! Don't look down, damn it. Keep your eyes and mind on the ledge I'm standing on. You're very close to making it. Just stay there, and I'll try to come down and help you up."

The intervention worked. Dan broke out of his trance, looked up, and started making his way, very, very cautiously, towards his friends. His pride overcame his fear. He wouldn't need anybody's help to reach safety. If his friends could cope with this challenge, then, damn it, so could he. Soon, he came close enough to the ledge to allow the others to pull him up, just moments before lightning hit the rock somewhere below again, causing the entire small grotto to vibrate.

"It wasn't acrophobia. I think it was simply an overwhelming general fear of dying," Dan explained, after regaining his breath. "I never saw horizontal lightning like this before."

"Heck, I'm not an expert on this either. I guess the gods of Bandits' Mountain regard us as cheeky intruders… But we're not that easy to dispose of," said Alex, with a relieved smile.

"Let's not get overly confident here," cautioned Victor. "We were very lucky so far, that's all. If this storm lasts for a long time, we're going to have to make some uncomfortable decisions about what to do next."

"I'm actually grateful for the whole damn thing. After we get back down, we'll have an even more vivid memory of the climb because of this great storm," declared Alex, who was in a strangely good mood.

"*If* we get back down…" said Victor grimly, while checking his glasses for signs of damage from the hail bombardment.

"I don't know about you, but I'm not planning to grow old in this cave… Of course, we'll get down, one way or another. Either on our own feet, or simply because of gravity," said Alex.

"Thanks for offering to help me out," Dan remembered.

"Ah, think nothing of it. Actually, I was mostly concerned about our backpacks down below. If you fell and landed on my stuff, I would have needed to buy expensive new gear, and I'm sort of low on cash, right now. Besides, if you die, who else would carry the tent the rest of the way?"

17

The prolonged storm forced them to spend an uncomfortable night shivering in the cold small cave, high up on the exposed north side of the mountain, without any food or blankets.

"Don't fall asleep, or you may never wake up," Alex advised.

They stayed awake by engaging in heated discussions about subjects such as extreme hypothermia and its possibly lethal consequences (by the time you have it, can you still be aware of that fact?), and which of the two female singers from ABBA was better looking. Victor and Dan were partial to Frida, the brunette with the lower, softer voice, while Alex favored Agnetha, the beautiful blonde whose higher and more dramatic voice seemed to take the lead in a majority of the group's songs. They argued about these and other such difficult-to-settle matters, with a passion that far exceeded the real importance of the topics to them, because the arguments helped in keeping them somewhat warm and distracted.

But in the early morning, just as they were about to contemplate the depressing prospect of having to stay up in the cave for another few hours, skipping breakfast in the process, the torrential rain simply stopped, and the dark clouds vanished as suddenly as they had arrived. The young men took advantage of the unexpected opportunity and in less than thirty minutes, they made their way past a treacherous overhanging cliff and found themselves standing on top of the highest peak they had ever climbed.

"Today, Bandits' Mountain! Tomorrow, Mont Blanc!" they shouted in unison, and then raised their arms triumphantly, high above their heads, like three Olympic athletes sharing the top step of the podium. Luckily, Alex's old camera was still relatively dry and working well enough, and the moment was recorded, if not quite for posterity, then at least for future reference.

From the unrivalled top of this small corner of their world, they could see many of the landmarks of their journey: the shepherd's small hut — a brown dot on the vast gray-green landscape, the black exit from the Bears' Cave, the soft shades of yellow of the dying tall grasses of the Valley of the Vipers, the silver twin waterfalls, which appeared motionless and silent in the distance, and even the outline of the little village, far below. Much closer, on top of the overhanging cliff, there was a very large and recently abandoned nest of a golden eagle. Even though the storm had blown away some of the branches making up the outer rim of the nest, the clean white bones of small rodents were still clearly visible among the tangled twigs on the inside. From their lofty vantage point, they also saw an easier way of getting back down, along the western side of the mountain, to the valley and their backpacks. Going down was, in many ways, much less challenging than the ascent, except for the fact that, this time, they had to face the dizzying precipice, instead of the solid mountain wall.

"The secret is to keep your butt as close to the ground as possible without scraping it on a sharp rock," Victor advised Dan, who seemed a bit hesitant before the inevitable descent.

"And don't worry about the mud. Your pants are already disgustingly filthy," added Alex.

As they came closer to the valley and around the western flank of the mountain, they were shocked to discover the huge one-eyed brown bear sniffing their backpacks. They abruptly stopped their descent, breathless, suspended about one hundred meters above their intended destination, and they watched in amazement as the bear, no doubt aware of their presence, carefully rummaged through Dan's rucksack, picked up the huge piece of sweet cheese they had purchased from the shepherd, and walked away, unhurriedly, with the cheese tightly held in its powerful jaws.

"Oh, good. Really great," Alex observed bitterly. "First, we had to skip dinner last night, and now there goes one of the main components of our lunch! If I weren't so damn tired, I'd wrestle that fat inconsiderate bastard for the cheese."

None of them went down to the valley floor for a good fifteen or twenty minutes, until it became clear that the bear would not return. "If he also took the chocolate, I'll hunt him down and kill him," said Alex. Fortunately, nothing other than the sweet cheese was missing. However, they were well aware that the big, greedy bear might not be satisfied solely with their cheese. As a result, not surprisingly, they gathered all their scattered equipment with unseemly speed, and left the area in a rather hasty and undignified manner.

18

Fortesque, a calm sort of fellow with a stiff upper lip and impressively long whiskers, was usually active only at night. He must have been born free and made his way along the bottom of the faraway Amazon in his youth, because catfish of his kind had never been known to breed in captivity. Alex and Fortesque had been roommates for over fifteen years. It had been a mutually beneficial association. Alex derived strength from Fortesque's imperturbable daily stoicism, and Fortesque obtained food and attention from Alex (although Fortesque didn't seem to need the attention and had never been observed to eat anything; Alex used to joke that Fortesque must have been on a fifteen-year hunger strike to protest against his living conditions).

"Maybe he'll eat in your expert care," said Alex, days before his departure, upon giving Fortesque to Victor, who had kept many aquarium fish over the years. "I can't really travel with a catfish, so I have no choice but to let go of him."

"He seems to have been doing quite well with you, for many years. I hope the change won't affect him too much," Victor replied calmly, even though he was deeply touched by Alex's thoughtful parting gift.

"I know you'll take good care of him, as well. Nobody knows how long they can live. For all we know, he could get to be one hundred years old," said Alex.

"In that case, I'll keep it for you until your return," was Victor's reply.

Fortesque was peaceful and, despite his large size, never attacked other fish. At the same time, he was well protected from potential enemies by a strong defensive armor of bony plates and spines. He was durable, resilient, stable, and long-lived. He had many of the qualities Victor admired most.

If Fortesque was aware of the changes in his life, he wasn't letting on.

19

The next morning, they scrambled up a steep rocky slope, covered by stunted junipers and rhododendrons, in order to reach a barely visible path, which stretched in front of them, like a tightrope awaiting a balancing act, along a very narrow ridge. The slowly rising, thickening fog prevented them from enjoying the spectacular views, over the steep precipices found on both sides of the thin trail. They were now in the realm of the mountain goats. Alex, who was leading the way, had to look constantly ahead, careful not to lose sight of the narrow path in the fog. He knew that even one misstep could plunge him instantly into the abyss. The others quietly followed Alex through the unsettling white waves of vapor, trying hard not to lose their nerve and concentration. The cold air sank deeper into their lungs after every breath, leaving behind little icicles of anxiety in the middle of their chests.

After a seemingly endless, tense walk along the jagged ridge, they started their descent, slowly, through the hollow interior of a gigantic chimney-like vertical tunnel carved by the water in the sandstone cliff wall. The first phase of their perilous descent, along the slippery walls of the natural chimney, ended when they reached a small flat ledge precariously perched above the abyss. The suspended shelf was adorned by clumps of the rare, velvety edelweiss flowers. On the adjacent lichen-covered rock wall, they found the small metal cross. It marked the spot where, almost exactly one year earlier, the rescue team had found Gabriel's bruised and frozen body.

They stood on the ledge, in the cold wind, and they bowed their heads, as a brief silent tribute to their old friend.

There was anger in Alex's voice — not the scornful kind of anger he reserved for the repressive regime, but a more reproachful, aching type — when he finally spoke: "What do you suppose could have possessed a really bright and talented guy like Gabriel to climb these dangerous peaks all alone, in his condition? Why would he do it?"

Victor tried to soften the harshness of the unanswered questions:

"He was a good mountaineer… But he was also terribly unlucky. The snow came unusually early over these peaks last year…"

"Poor Gabriel was always unlucky. In that sense, he was Alex's opposite," added Dan, riding on the crest of a wave of sudden compassion, which made him over-estimate the importance of bad luck, and bracing himself for Alex's reply.

Alex was usually not a great believer in luck and fate. He believed that frequent references to luck and bad luck tended to trivialize people's lives and diminish the significance of human thoughts and actions. Like many fortunate, confident people, he tended to downplay the role of good luck in his life. But, this time, his reply was fairly subdued, by his standards:

"He wasn't always unlucky, damn it! He had real talent. He had a beautiful Norwegian girlfriend who really cared for him. He had friends willing to help. And, after all, we both survived that close encounter with the farm bear equally unscathed. We both walked away with our futures still intact."

"But that was only because you must have had enough good fortune for two on that fateful trip," concluded Victor with unassailable common sense. "That's one of the reasons why it's good to have you around on these journeys."

The mild compliment was received, but, uncharacteristically, Alex did not re-ply to either half of that statement. Instead, he said, "He didn't tell me he was planning this. There was not even a hint. Had I known, I would have tried my best to talk him out of it, and if I couldn't do that, I would have joined him on that trip. It didn't have to end like this for him. Dying all alone, far from everyone. It's not even clear if he was killed by the fall or hypothermia."

"It was probably the fall. But they weren't sure. The rescuers couldn't get to him until several weeks later. The conditions were awful. They said this entire area was covered by a thick sheet of ice. They had to work for hours before they could finally remove his body. We can only hope it was quick, and he didn't suffer too much in those final moments," said Victor.

"If you could have the option of knowing the circumstances of your own death, would you choose to know?" asked Dan, suddenly changing the subject.

"Probably not," said Victor. "That kind of knowledge might spoil whatever amount of time I still have left among the living. I'd probably waste the whole time just waiting for, and imagining, the end. Who needs that?"

Dissatisfied with the answer, Dan pursued that line of questioning: "Don't you ever worry about not knowing?"

But Victor was being decidedly unhelpful: "I have enough worries already. Why add to the pile?"

"It wouldn't be so bad, if you found out that you're supposed to go gently, in your sleep, at the age of ninety," suggested Dan.

"Even then, knowing the end would somehow detract from the bittersweet mystery of the unfolding of one's life. It would take something away from the meaning of getting up each morning. We're never certain of anything, but we keep hoping for the best and plodding along. In a way, the small uncertainty keeps us going. It's always there, in the background, and we learn to live with it. We have no choice. And there are many other concerns — big or small. You run to catch the bus in the morning because you're trying not to be late for work. You wash your hands to keep from getting sick. You have to get through each day. There is no way to know the future. You can anticipate, but you cannot be sure. If I knew I had a guaranteed long life ahead of me, I might find myself more complacent and unfocused, for example," replied Victor, still not persuaded, and hoping to give his definitive answer to all those unsettling questions.

Alex added, defiantly, "Heck, I think I can manage to be quite complacent and unfocused even without that kind of grim knowledge. Are we supposed to be grateful to be given access to limited knowledge of our pre-assigned dead ends? Victor gets stifling old age; Dan gets an early fatal anxiety attack… This kind of ridiculous notion implies that there is a certain inevitability about the way in which each of us is supposed to make the final exit from this world. I cannot accept that. Sometimes, there are things we can do to either postpone or at least change our own demise. If I found out, for the sake of argument, that I'm supposed to die by falling out of the giant Ferris wheel at the amusement park, for instance, you can bet that I would never get anywhere near an amusement park ever again! In that way, this knowledge could certainly make a difference."

"If Gabriel had known, do you think he could have stayed away from these mountains?" asked Dan.

"Probably not…" answered Alex softly, looking intently at the small iron cross, surrounded by the little clumps of fragile alpine flowers.

20

Alex's thoughts drifted briefly to a fragment from one of the last conversations he had had with Gabriel. They had just come out of a theater after watching a rather mediocre Western, and Gabriel asked: "What is your favorite friendship from any of the movies you've seen?"

"Han Solo and Chewbacca, of course," Alex replied.

"And I suppose you think of yourself as Han Solo?" asked Gabriel again.

"You said it, Chewie," answered Alex with a smile, and then they went into a small pizza place for lunch. After they each had two big slices, there was one more piece left, and Alex insisted that Gabriel should have it. That was the best pizza Alex could ever remember tasting.

Gabriel had been Alex's best friend — someone Alex could always count on, the same way Han Solo could always rely on Chewbacca. Only, Chewbacca was big, strong, and long-lived, and Gabriel had been fragile, and was now gone.

21

Gabriel sat motionless in front of Alex's silent one-hundred-and-fifty-year-old piano, and tried to think of his music. But the melodies stubbornly refused to come out of their secret hiding places. For more than two hours, he could only manage to remember a few easy pieces he had learned in his childhood from his very first piano teacher (a once-famous elderly musician reduced to giving private lessons in order to survive). Even the melancholy *Für Elise*, which he used to be able to perform flawlessly at the age of eight (that performance had even earned him the first prize in a municipal talent contest), could now only come to him in strangely disjointed tiny fragments.

Gabriel would not be able to recall his own music, but he could easily imagine what the future held in store for someone in his situation. Unable to finish his studies and improve his playing, forbidden from leaving the country even for brief trips to neighboring regions, he would constantly be on the move, from one dismal construction site to another, always expected to perform the most menial tasks available. Eventually, if everything would progress unexpectedly well, the most he could ever hope for would be the permission to play in some workers' club, for a perpetually inebriated and indifferent audience. Most people would wisely avoid him, and others might once again take an interest in him for the wrong reasons. His few close friends would inevitably get on with their lives and move on to better things. They still had some options and some real hopes.

Ultimately, as Alex had often said, one had to be self-reliant. Trusting others, that was Gabriel's big mistake. He had naively thought that, by bribing an old railway worker he knew, he could guarantee himself a problem-free passage across the border. Just to be on the safe side, he had also tried to appeal to that man's compassion, by opening up and explaining his reasons for leaving in simple and straightforward words. The worker, who seemed reliable and had a firm handshake and a steady gaze, took the substantial bribe without hesitation. But then he must have immediately turned around and denounced Gabriel to the authorities.

They knew exactly where to look. They showed no hesitation and no surprise. It was the beginning of the nightmare. He attempted to explain that he was not trying to cause any trouble or publicize the plight of his people elsewhere. He was simply an anonymous student hoping to start a new life on his own, away from the spotlight. But his anonymity did not provide any protection. On the contrary, his anonymous status probably made him even more vulnerable. Nobody on the outside knew of his imprisonment, and nobody could intervene on his behalf. No moderating influence could restrain the hounds. Like many others, he was at his captors' fickle mercy. At least that branch of the government was working efficiently, most of the time.

The situation was very different for Alex, whose parents had fled to the West several years ago. They were now well-established professors at a prestigious Western university, and they had started a determined international letter writing campaign among fellow academics, lobbying for a passport for their only son. That risky campaign, which threw Alex straight into the glare of the authorities' spotlight, could have backfired badly, but in the end, it didn't. Alex would eventually get his passport. Deep down, he always must have felt he had a real chance of achieving his goals, and that conviction was often reflected in his defiant words. The dictatorship they had spent their whole lives under was not always confident enough to withstand high-profile, organized international pressure. Thousands of professors, from dozens of democratic countries, had signed the letter urging the authorities to set Alex free. The Helsinki Accords, which their country had signed on to but never abided by, were invoked in the letter, among other things. The Accords included respect for human rights and fundamental freedoms, but in their country, there was no freedom of speech — no freedom of thought openly expressed in any form, really, no freedom of the press, and, as Gabriel was painfully aware, also no freedom to travel outside the fortified borders of their land. Alex was strong and outspoken, but with international backing and without having known any major setbacks or any time in prison, he could afford to be.

Still, Gabriel admired Alex's prodigious strength of character. One incident in particular stood out, even after all that time. Despite his fading overall memory, he remembered well that terrifying bear encounter, when Alex bravely stood his ground, without even flinching. Alex's uncommon bravery prevented Gabriel from running away. After all, he couldn't run and let his brave friend down. If necessary, they would have fought that big bear together, shoulder to shoulder, like brothers.

Alex had always been a true friend. He was the first one who called after the prison sentence finally ended. Shortly after that phone call, when Gabriel met Alex in a coffee shop (where coffee could no longer be found), they both started laughing, while trying to guess which of the new customers at the nearby tables had been assigned to spy on them. Alex was convinced he had identified his new shadow (he had used the shadow's exceedingly narrow forehead as the decisive clue), while Gabriel couldn't really find his. Gabriel did not feel he needed a new shadow anymore, even though he had lost his old one in a long-forgotten dream. They laughed hard, with the obvious relief of people who know they are on their way out, moving away from previous rules and commitments. Nobody else could have helped Gabriel laugh that day. Yes, Alex was a very good friend, and he deserved a very good life.

Gabriel knew he had to take a much-needed break from it all. He wanted a long rest and some quiet time to think, on his own, away from the city and far away from any walls. At that moment, as tiny fragments of forgotten music started to briefly coalesce into rediscovered melodies, Gabriel first thought of a solitary journey to the silent faraway mountains.

22

They continued their descent for several more hours without allowing themselves any more periods of rest. At the foot of the mountain, they suddenly came across the twisted, rusty wreckage of a military helicopter. Alex was getting ready to take a picture of the unexpected find, but Victor advised against it.

"I wouldn't do that," he said. "You never know."

Alex paused for a few seconds, and then he put his camera away, without using it.

"It's probably too dark here, anyway. Too much shade," he explained.

In their land of rumors and whispers, there were many official secrets and many other matters which were widely assumed to be secret, although nobody could be quite sure. Alex recalled visiting his grandmother's grave several years ago, during his childhood. As he walked through the cemetery, he saw about twenty or thirty identical new tombstones arranged in a row, side by side. They all honored young military pilots who had died on the same day, just a few months earlier. A major accident had to have taken place, and yet no news about this incident had been reported.

They walked away from the imposing massif, leaving the harsh wind behind, and continued through the mature coniferous forest before reaching the aptly named Valley of the Flowers. Alex recognized many of the eye-catching flowering plant species and even the more modestly attired grasses, having seen them all years ago, dried, pressed, and carefully identified, in his grandfather's impressive herbarium.

Sunny sky-blue chicories and slightly darker bluebells interspersed with red and white clover, purple self-heal, golden alpine buttercups, and blood-red field poppies provided bright specks of color on the vivid, healthy green background of the valley floor. The notorious nettle plants, with their small white or purple flowers,

and the stinging, rash-inducing leaves Dan had a rare talent for frequently brush-
ing against, could be seen growing in small patches, scattered among the grasses,
seemingly at random. The wild chamomile flowers and the ox-eye daisies, looking
like three-dimensional versions of the suns Alex used to draw as a child (at the
center of his always light blue skies), were found mostly around the edges of the
valley, farther from the mossy banks of the temporary brook in the middle.

The little brook meandered peacefully over most of the field, crossing the path
ahead in several places. From a distance, the flowers looked like multicolored dots
carefully deployed on a huge impressionist canvas. A canvas too large to be confined within the walls of any art gallery. The closer they got, the more they detected
the delicate movements of the impressionist dots, slowly rocked by a gentle breeze,
which seemed uncertain about its final destination. The encroaching early autumn
had so far spared the bright summer colors of the valley. A beautiful oasis in the
harsh, chilly alpine desert.

The caraway plants were also there, another small part of the delicate ecosystem
of the fragile oasis, almost invisible among their colorful neighbors. The thin, black
caraway seeds, which Alex used to gather during his summer trips to mountain
meadows, formed the main ingredient of a healing kind of soup, which was said
to chase away most abdominal pains. Alex had sampled that natural remedy during
the rare occasions when his shark stomach (as Victor had called it) had let him
down. Lurking among the skinny caraway stems loaded with soothing seeds, the
lacy leaves of the poison hemlock ("the black sheep of the carrot family," as Alex's
grandfather had described it) offered a very different type of herbal remedy, for
very different types of problems.

They stopped near a curious, mushroom-shaped outcrop, which stood alone in
the middle of the valley, and rested their sore backs against the cool surface of the
giant rock.

"I believe this structure is called the Old Lady," said Dan.

"It doesn't look anything like an old woman," Victor responded, obviously
puzzled.

"Maybe it did, hundreds or thousands of years ago, when they named it," explained Dan.

"Or maybe the old ladies really used to be quite different in these parts — you know, fat, gray and cold," said Alex.

"Is there anything more annoying than mosquito bites on sunburned skin?" asked Dan, looking at the red bumps on his now bright pink left forearm.

"Yes, the people who whine about it," answered Alex. "We're all sunburned and covered with mosquito bites. It's part of the 'fun' of being out here. At least, I must have killed dozens of mosquitoes during this trip, so far. There's a price to pay for taking a bite out of me."

"I can't believe the summer is almost over, already. September is a cruel month, which always arrives much too quickly. Every year, this takes me by surprise, somehow. Each June I have all these hopeful plans for the summer — I'll read ten great books, I'll relax, I'll get in shape, I'll sort out my life, and all that. And each time, not much gets done. Fall colors aside, autumn really stinks," said Dan, staring at the yellowing leaves of a nearby bush.

"And how many more years do you think you'll need, before you'll be able to get over it?" Alex inquired.

"This summer appears to have been even shorter than the ones before. Did you notice that? Time really seems to fly faster and faster, these days. Where does it all go, so very fast? I feel like I'm on a roller coaster, forever accelerating, to nowhere," Dan went on, leaving Alex's question largely unanswered.

"I have been told that's a sure sign of advanced aging," teased Alex.

Dan, however, took the light comment quite seriously: "It may be true, you know. As a kid, I thought that the period of time between two consecutive Christmas holidays was really long. Not anymore! Nowadays, there's one Christmas after another, at the speed of light."

"Obviously, you were looking forward to Christmas much more as a child. That's probably all there is to it," said Victor, adopting a professorial tone.

"Well, Danny, if you're worried about time going by too fast, there's always the army life. According to Gabriel, each week of military service tends to be of the endless variety. And those twenty-two months I've spent waiting for the initial approval to emigrate didn't quite fly by either, truth be told," added Alex.

"Those are good points. They really are. But nothing changes the fact that in only ten short days I'll have to start another unbearable year of lousy med school courses. Incredible! It seems as if I just finished last year's final exams yesterday. I'm just not ready, guys," concluded Dan.

"If your theory of accelerating time is correct, this school year should go by faster than the previous one. You're going to be a doctor in no time. You'll become a pillar of the community. So, you might as well try to relax," said Victor, determined to help Dan feel better.

"I can't relax. Didn't Alex once say that no decent man should want to be a pillar of this community?"

"Why should those words apply to you?" joked Alex.

"In all seriousness," Dan continued, without even glancing at Alex, "this is going to be one tough year from start to finish. Every grade counts. Each examination could determine the course of my career. The better the grades the bigger the city I may be sent to after I graduate — if I graduate, that is. And I heard that it helps to be married and have a kid before graduation, as well. Graduates with families get better assignments. I'll probably end up in some remote village without paved roads and electricity, where I'll have to walk for miles each day to get water from some contaminated well."

"Sounds like fun," said Alex.

"You don't know what it's like. It's hard to make friends in med school. Everybody is so competitive and so obsessed with getting those top grades, no matter what. You get the feeling they would sell their mothers for a slightly higher grade, if they could. And, from what I heard, some of the new professors should be even more self-important and sadistic than the old ones. I didn't think that could be possible. They enjoy showing off and humiliating students like me. To top it all off, I believe I'll have to do my first two weeks of apprenticeship in the psychiatry ward this fall," said Dan.

"Good. Don't forget to say hello to all our good friends there," Alex reminded him.

"All this effort, all this stress, and I'm not even sure I like the idea of becoming a doctor. I just couldn't think of any other viable alternative careers. And then, there was the family pressure: 'Wouldn't it be great if our son became a doctor?', 'What could be better?', 'Dr. Dan has a nice ring to it,' and all that kind of stuff. Some of my colleagues seemed to have always known they wanted to be doctors — apparently, even during infancy, before they could walk and talk, or while still in the womb, in some cases. I never had that kind of certainty. I still don't. What if I get the diagnosis wrong? A headache could mean anything from a cold to a tumor. And let's not even talk about the multiple possible causes of pain in the abdominal region. At least, I'll be very busy, most of the time — my lousy life will be over before I know it," continued Dan, absent-mindedly.

"Well, the uncertainty about the diagnosis is one reason why I never wanted to be a doctor. That, and not wanting to spend my whole life in hospitals. Normally, you would think most people would want to avoid those places at all costs. The stench of sickness and disinfectants, the worried people, the crazy hours. Both of my uncles were doctors, and they were always summoned to the hospital — even at night or on Sundays. The phone rang, and off they went. One time, I think one of them forgot an instrument inside a patient he had performed surgery on, hours earlier. So, he had to operate again, to retrieve his forceps, or whatever else he left in there. I'm not sure if the patient survived, but on the bright side, the forceps were as good as new. Can't imagine why anyone would choose to do this for a living," said Alex.

"It's supposed to be a noble profession, if it's done right," mentioned Dan, without much conviction.

"Perhaps, but, even if you're in it for all the right reasons, you still have to sacrifice a good part of your life to attend to others. Call me selfish and callous, if you must, but I just cannot see myself doing that every day. Besides, it doesn't seem like a very creative pursuit, most of the time. Let's say you're a surgeon, and you have three appendectomies and two gallstone removal procedures on the schedule, or other such things, each day. In a way, it's like you're some sort of a plumber of the human body. Not much of an intellectual exercise," said Alex.

"Some of my colleagues would really disagree with you, but I am not sure I can," Dan replied. "Maybe I just don't have what it takes to be a doctor, after all. It's quite possible I have been wasting my time."

"Perhaps a new girlfriend would help," suggested Alex.

"I don't think so. They always leave me after a while, anyway. Apparently, I just don't have that much to offer, and I think I had just about enough rejection to last me for quite some time," said Dan.

That naked display of self-doubt and honesty seemed like a suitable end to that part of the conversation — it didn't appear there was anything else to add — so Alex turned towards Victor, instead: "And how about you, Vic? What's next for you?"

"Nothing spectacular, really," came the predictable reply. "I'll just do my best to get by, hopefully without having to make too many petty compromises. That would be my definition of success. I guess the easiest way to achieve this is probably by keeping quiet, unassuming, and away from any spotlights."

"How are you going to manage that?" Alex enquired again. "After all, you're a born entertainer."

"Don't be such a smart ass," cautioned Victor, without a trace of rancor in his even voice.

"That's your future father-in-law talking," added Alex with a smile, before Victor went on.

"Unlike you, I'm planning a life on a small scale. A quiet life — without making a fuss over everything. I'm going to continue to be a good provider for my pet tropical fish. I'll try not to lose my appreciation for the little sources of joy: a good book once in a while, the weekly football games, perhaps the odd play, a piece of good cheese. And I'll insulate myself from all the rest, if I can. As you like to say, at least we'll always have the mountains… It's still a beautiful country out here."

"Don't forget to mail me the local football scores, from time to time. It's unlikely I'll be able to find them in Canadian newspapers."

"You know you can count on me."

23

Like the others, although maybe a little less than Alex did, Victor admired the West, and longed to travel there and see the important places he could only read about. The monuments of ancient Greece — the birthplace of democracy — were not even that far away, yet Greece and its ancient democratic ideals seemed so very difficult to reach. And Rome, a place where he could understand the language and see Decebal's anguished face, frozen in the white marble of Trajan's column, was only slightly farther, but just as difficult to get to.

To a much greater degree than Alex, however, Victor felt insecure and uncertain about leaving his homeland, relatives, and friends behind, possibly forever. He felt an acute sense of loss even thinking about a potential separation from the physical setting of all his memories and his roots. For better or worse, and lately, he had to admit, it had been mostly for the worse, this was his home. The only home he had ever known. If every good person would depart, what would become of it? What hope could there be for the future? Even in the worst situations, only a small minority could ever leave. The vast majority always stayed behind and took the consequences. And Silvia would never agree to go away. She was much more comfortable as a dutiful member of the majority. Besides, her father would almost certainly lose his important job and social standing if she ever left.

Victor was not oblivious to the many problems all around. He disliked a lot of things, of course, and even indulged in a bit of complaining, when he was alone with his few trusted friends. Most of all, he hated the strange visit he had received a few months earlier. As he arrived at his apartment door, and was about to get the key out of his pocket, two people emerged from the obscurity of the unlit corridor. There they stood in front of him, a middle-aged couple with black hats and matching beige overcoats, looking somewhat like Bogart and Bacall, only without the style and the glamour. They had come to ask him about Alex. They wanted to know what Alex was "really like." Did he ever get drunk? Did he smoke? Was he a gambler? What were his main weak spots? Was he dating several young women at the same time? Any ideas on who those girlfriends might be? Any other immoral or anti-social tendencies? Did Alex talk much about the outside world, these days? How about the world within their borders? Politics, perhaps? Were all the rumors true? They already had a lot of relevant information, they reassured Victor, but they just needed to confirm a few more small details. Nothing really important. Just for the sake of a complete record, that's all. They had a job to do, after all, surely Victor could understand that, but they would, of course, guarantee that any information he could provide would be kept strictly confidential. Alex would never know.

"Cooperation could be very important to you, comrade, especially in your situation," the man said to Victor, in a cold, formal voice.

Victor wondered exactly what situation the Bogart impersonator was referring to. The upcoming draft? Making trouble at his workplace? Possible problems with Silvia's teaching job assignment? Were they really serious, or was it all a bluff? At the end of a long day, Victor felt too tired to care.

"We could help you," the woman said, with an enigmatic, joyless smile.

Victor took a deep breath and adjusted his glasses.

"If you don't mind," he said slowly, "I would rather help myself." And then he closed the apartment door quite abruptly, without inviting them in.

With the economy in the toilet, and shortages all around, they can still afford to hire an army of rejects to read everybody's mail, tap everybody's phone, and compile useless files on many good people, Victor thought, while feeling his forehead overheat, upon remembering the unsavory incident. It was not enough that he had to deal with incompetents at work, and then, after all that unpaid overtime spent fixing other people's stupid mistakes, he had to line up for hours just to get a few basic groceries. They were now coming to harass him at home. There was no sanctuary left, no dividing line, and no more restraint. Sometimes, it would have been easy to give in to anger.

But he also believed (and he couldn't say this in front of Alex, for fear of being ridiculed) that it was his duty to stay and make the best of it. At least, even Alex had to agree, theirs was a beautiful land. The mountains and the sea, the hills and the lakes, the vast ancient forests, four gentle seasons almost equal in length, many regions still relatively unspoiled. There was still plenty to be grateful for. Victor wasn't at all sure he could really belong anywhere else. He might learn to adjust to other worlds, but he would probably never truly belong there.

Alex longed to write his hard-hitting novels from afar, to take the glory and the risks, to record every detail for posterity, and repay every bill, with plenty of interest. He was driven by a thirst for revenge. Alex frequently expressed regret that the title *Les Misérables* had already been used, since it would have been perfect for his first novel. But, Victor thought, posterity is an illusion we hang onto because of our inability to really grasp our own mortality and insignificance and the illogical randomness of life. This illusion, which can lead to the deeply felt unhappiness of unfulfilled great expectations, can be entertaining and keep us busy for a while, but it is only an illusion, nevertheless. It was the illusion that sustained Alex and nourished the strength of his convictions. The fanciful notion that what we do always matters, and that we can change destiny and defy the passage of time if only we try hard enough and have enough willpower. Alex was becoming an outsider already. Perhaps he had always been destined to be one.

Victor, like most of his compatriots, knew the quest to influence the major social and political events of their troubled homeland would not only be futile, at least in the short run, but also quite dangerous. Everything is temporary, and, in due course, even this increasingly erratic dictatorship would pass into well-deserved oblivion. They were most likely living through the tail end of the repression, although no one could be really sure just how long that tail end would turn out to be. As Alex had put it: "Even after the head of the monster is gone, the tail may keep on thrashing and twitching for quite some time."

But Victor was determined to remain loyal to his own cherished hopes for as long as necessary. The trick was not to actively try to escape into the unknown, but to passively attempt to outlast the rough times. The wise "turtle strategy." Victor did not regard his attitude as fatalistic. There were certain things he cared deeply about. He knew he would fight, quietly, to keep his integrity, on a small, private scale, and raise his kids well. His kids would certainly grow up to see a time when integrity would be in fashion again, right here, in their rightful home. And, perhaps, that would be the most important reward of all. One day, Victor's kids would be able to read Alex's novels in their original language. They wouldn't have to smuggle Alex's books into their country, after rare brief trips abroad. They wouldn't even understand all the reasons behind Alex's angry, cutting lines. It was a dream worth waiting for. Victor would be there — an old man by then, perhaps — for Alex's return. It would be his small personal victory over time and destiny. He would survive and endure in his very own home, with his familiar hobbies and mannerisms, surrounded by the few important people in his life and the few remaining precious family heirlooms. The quiet joy of continuity. Real happiness, after all, does not lie in epic events, but in the small details of daily life. That has to be the same all over the world, he thought.

Unlike Dan, Victor did not envy Alex's undeniable new opportunities (and the accompanying greater risks of failure). But he did envy — although he couldn't fully understand — Alex's unshakeable certainty that a better life would be waiting elsewhere.

24

Shortly after the end of the brief period of rest, they left the beautiful clearing and reentered the forest. The conifers were gradually giving way to impressive stands of giant, time-defying, oak and beech trees. They followed the nicely shaded path through the forest until they reached an abandoned orchard. It looked like a good place for a somewhat longer stopover, and they decided to finish their remaining food supplies at the edge of the forest, among the old, gnarled apple trees.

"Here, we can at least enjoy some fresh apples for dessert," said Victor, who was eager for a more substantial break, after all that walking.

"That's true enough. It's just too bad we seem to be lacking a main course, though. Man can't live on apples and coffee alone. At least, not this man," added Alex, feeling rather undernourished.

"Well, we still have a bit of sausage left, if you're brave enough, but I have to warn you that I tried some last night, and it tastes like horse dung," said Dan.

"I'm curious, do you often eat horse dung? Or just on special occasions? I mean, how would you know what that tastes like?" probed Alex.

"I was only trying to help. I felt it was my duty as a medical student to prevent you from getting sick. We've taken enough chances already. It would be a shame to end up with a severe case of food poisoning," concluded Dan, a bit hurt that his noble intentions were made fun of.

"I appreciate the concern, but I don't want to end up with a severe case of starvation either, doctor. So, if you don't mind, and if you don't intend to keep it all for yourself, just give me whatever is left of the damn sausage!" said Alex.

"Fine. Just don't blame me for the consequences," said Dan. "At least, there's probably not enough of it left to kill you."

Alex cut a small piece of the remaining sausage, put it in his mouth, chewed slowly for a while, and then declared: "I must admit you're right. It is terrible. Possibly the worst I've ever had. You wouldn't happen to have some more though, would you?"

Since, on this last day of their trip, they were running a bit short of both food and time, they decided to combine lunch and supper into a single meal, strategically scheduled for the middle of the afternoon.

The strategic meal was briefly interrupted by the sudden appearance of a graceful, ghostly-white horse at the edge of the forest. After watching the horse silently for a little while, they tried to tempt it with an assortment of freshly picked apples. But the stallion seemed weary of strangers and did not accept the small gifts. As Alex tried to come near, the white horse turned around and ran back into the forest, towards the mountains.

They couldn't explain what the horse was doing there, alone, far away from the nearest farms. Furthermore, it seemed obvious that the elegant, independent stallion had never been a beast of burden on any farm. Other impossible-to-answer questions remained. For how long had the horse survived on its own in the harsh environment at the edge of the mountains? Where did it come from? Such an unusually beautiful specimen would always be a conspicuous and coveted target. Could it keep dodging attacks by bears in the summer and wolf packs in the winter? Could it avoid being driven too close to the villages, where the locals would surely try to capture it and condemn it to the indignities of life as a workhorse? Would a life spent tied up, either to a carriage, or a plough, or a wooden pole in a stable, be preferable to the constant risk of deadly attacks by savage predators on exposed mountain meadows? They knew they couldn't do anything to help, but somehow, they felt happy to know that the now invisible horse was there, untamed, running free through the dark forest. They agreed to classify the brief, sudden apparition as a minor mystery, and they chose to treat themselves to the small green apples the stallion had rejected.

25

At the end of their last meal near the mountains, they lingered in the old orchard, unwilling to walk away too soon.

"Well, I guess our journey is almost over," said Dan, with sincere regret. "Who knows when, or even if, we'll see these mountains again?"

"He's the one leaving," mentioned Victor, pointing his head towards Alex, "not you."

"I was referring to all of us, as a group," Dan specified. "Who knows when we'll all be here again, at the same time? Maybe never."

"I see that you are both specializing in stating the obvious, these days," mentioned Alex. "Let's not get melodramatic. We're still here now, and we can all return to this place again, at least in theory."

"Do you think you'll ever return?" asked Dan.

"I don't know. The truth is, I really hate the idea of flying, especially over long distances. But I'm sure I'll think of this place often, for many years to come. So, in that sense, yes, I will return," Alex answered.

"I didn't know you hated flying," said Victor.

"What's there to like about it? You're strapped in a chair for hours, and you have absolutely no control over your life during this entire time. And you have to trust that none of the pilots, or fellow passengers, or the people who check the plane before it takes off, are drunk, drugged, or insane, and that the weather will be acceptable, and nobody spills coffee over the control panels, and no birds get near the engines, and a million other things. It seems even worse than the truck that brought us to the mountains — at least that truck's wheels were in contact with the ground, most of the time," said Alex.

"I am quite confident you'll survive the experience," said Victor.

"What do you mean 'quite confident'? Couldn't you at least lie to me and tell me you were sure I'll make it?"

"Would that have helped?"

"Of course not. But I would have appreciated the good intentions."

Dan did not pay much attention to this exchange, and he seemed unable to break out of his sadness, as he said:

"You know, it's funny, but when I first came here, years ago, I used to think that these mountains were very far away from home."

"They *are* very far from home," said Victor. "Once we get to the nearest town, it will take us fourteen hours by train to get back. Alex will spend less time on his flights to Canada than we will on the train."

"No more talk of airplanes, please. I just ate. And my stomach is fighting hard to process that damn sausage," cautioned Alex, lightly tapping his abdomen.

"I've never even been on a plane," said Dan. "I've never been anywhere, really."

"Well, you're here now, and tomorrow you'll be back home, and life will go on," said Alex, rather impatiently.

"You're both missing the point. I'm not sure I still feel at home anywhere in this land," said Dan.

Even though he was still flanked by his two best friends, Dan felt alone already. For many years, during their get-togethers, he had felt like a pendulum, constantly swinging between Alex's fiery flights of fancy and Victor's down-to-earth caution. He envied them both for being able to remain unintimidated in front of their very different, but equally uncertain, future paths. Two men who knew what they wanted and were ready for the consequences. Dan could boast of no such confidence. He felt lost in front of his own constantly bifurcating road ahead, paralyzed by the feeling of not knowing what to do and which way to turn. He couldn't decide whether he should try to reach a truce with his surroundings and accept his fate, the way Victor seemed to have done, or follow Alex's lead, and attempt to start a new life, a very different life, somewhere else, far away. Either way, how could he be sure he wouldn't be making an irreparable mistake? It was useless to struggle with that kind of unfair choice. Dan knew that, for the time being at least, he lacked the courage of following either path. He felt certain he was destined to remain immobile, and increasingly unsettled, as his youth and his opportunities for reaching a meaningful decision slipped away, at an ever-accelerating speed. His friends were getting on with the rest of their lives, leaving him behind. He could imagine the emptiness of walking the familiar streets of their hometown, or the mountain paths, without the people he grew up with and came to trust.

After a respectful pause, Victor looked at his watch, as discreetly as he could, and felt compelled to ask a couple of practical questions: "What's the plan for this evening? How are we getting home?"

"We should be able to find a truck on the old forestry road, just behind the next hill. If we can manage to convince the driver to take us there, we should reach the nearest town just in time to catch the night train to the capital," answered Dan.

26

A few weeks after Gabriel's disappearance in the cold, distant mountains, Gabriel's uncle, the engineer, hung a white bed sheet from the balcony of his small suburban apartment. The sheet advertised a simple message: "Give us passports, not lies," carefully written in red paint — the only color available in the department store that week.

Until that Sunday morning, Gabriel's uncle had never done anything even remotely controversial, except, perhaps, for turning up the volume a bit, while listening to his treasured jazz tapes. Otherwise, he had always been a quiet man, and his only discernible interests, aside from jazz, were football, crossword puzzles, and stamp collecting.

It took a little while for the first passers-by to look up and notice that this was not a bed sheet like any of the other ones, which were drying out in the sun, in neighboring balconies.

"What is that, written on the sheet?" the little boy who first looked up asked.

"Something about getting a passport," his slightly older brother whispered.

"Daddy, what's a passport?" the little boy persisted.

"I don't know son," his father joked. "I never saw one."

Several people nearby, who were gathered around an outdoor chess table, laughed and winked, causing the father to stop smiling, take his boys by the hand, and walk away in a hurry.

After that, everything happened very fast. The dark van came, and a few grim-faced men got out. They knocked down the apartment door, removed the incriminating bed sheet, broke a vase or two while stumbling around the living room, and used unnecessary force as they roughly escorted Gabriel's uncle out of the apartment and down the staircase. It was all over so quickly that many witnesses could not even be sure the entire incident took place at all. An overturned little cactus, with its roots sticking defiantly upwards, was left behind, to slowly die in the middle of the thick living room carpet.

The small apartment with the broken door remained unoccupied for a very long time.

27

In the late evening, they stepped off the truck in the middle of an ugly, industrial town built around the giant smelter. All the street lights were turned off, but plenty of thick smoke still rose up from the tall stacks. Even though they were used to the pollution in the capital, they still found it hard to breathe the air near the smelter. A huge, faded banner, stretched across the main street and now barely visible in the crepuscular light, reminded the population that the five-year plan should be completed in four and a half years. The banner had probably been there for at least ten years.

"Back to civilization," said Alex, unable to resist his sarcastic impulses.

A kindly resident of the town helped them find their way, through the maze of dark streets, to the railway station.

Unable to see much, Alex banged his knee against a garbage bin, and couldn't suppress a scream of frustration followed by a few choice words about the local conditions. From across the street, two uniformed policemen pointed their flashlights at him, to get a better look at the source of the noise.

"Let's try not to attract too much attention. You never know with these guys," Victor whispered.

"I didn't think they would mind the sound of suffering," Alex replied, feeling his sore knee, and his defiant words alarmed his friends. Fortunately, however, the policemen walked away unconcerned, and disappeared in a nearby pub.

"Remember, we're not in the mountains anymore," Victor advised, quite sensibly.

But Alex wasn't quite finished just yet.

"Why are all the street lights off? Are we expecting a bombing raid anytime soon?" he asked, rhetorically.

"No sir, I think it's dark because of the cutbacks," said a nearby luggage porter, unexpectedly.

"Tell me my good man, do you know when the eight o'clock train for the capital should actually arrive?" asked Alex.

"It usually arrives between ten and eleven at night, sir, but I heard they had some trouble with the track, up near the mountains, earlier today," came the earnest reply.

"Oh, I see... Thank you very much. We'll have more time to enjoy the surroundings, then."

28

The proud king, tired of trying to elude his inevitable destiny, dismounted and set his white horse free. The powerful stallion waited nearby for a little while, before receiving the subtle signal which sent him galloping through the poppy fields, across the beautiful valley and away from the approaching large group of soldiers. The weary king stood calmly in the shadow of an immense boulder which sprang unexpectedly from among the blood-red flowers. With the boulder at his back, he watched the columns of intruders growing larger in the horizon, as they slowly came forward, in steady pursuit. The soldiers were approaching him cautiously, from three sides, even though they were facing just one man.

The king could imagine his fate, if he were to allow himself to surrender. He would find himself dragged through the streets of Imperial Rome as a slave, chained together with his few surviving loyal chieftains (the others had either died in battle or sampled the poison hemlock remedy), behind one of emperor Trajan's many ostentatiously gilded chariots. The fanatical, hostile crowds lining the streets would focus most of their blistering derision on him, the former brave ruler of a formerly independent kingdom. After losing control over his kingdom, he would also lose control over his own life. He turned his head away from his suddenly insignificant enemies, for only a moment, to watch the graceful outline of the running white stallion disappear behind a nearby foothill. Then, Decebal, the last king of the Dacians, gripped his sword firmly and ran its cold blade over his jugular, without hesitation. The mortally wounded king kept standing, against the cool rock, with his eyes wide open and the sword still tightly in his hand, for a long time. As the intruding soldiers came near, the king finally fell, silently, to the ground. The poppies cushioned his fall, and instantly covered his body and his final resting place.

The soldiers looked for many hours, from one end of the valley to the other, but they could find neither the fallen king nor a suitable explanation for his sudden disappearance. Fearing their emperor's wrath, in case they returned without proof of Decebal's death, they cut off the head of a dead Dacian warrior, lying in a battlefield nearby, and took it back to Rome. The head of the simple warrior was proudly shown to the emperor and then paraded before the Senate, as if it were Decebal's.

Not long after the soldiers had stopped their futile search, a small mountain brook with very clear waters fought its way to the surface and came to light on the very spot where the mighty king had fallen. To this day, the clear waters of the spring can only be crossed by those who come with good intentions. Before all others, the brook would inexplicably widen, resembling a raging river during an early spring flood. Over time, even the soldiers who deliberately brought the wrong head to Rome chose to forget that the dead brave king had never left his beloved faraway mountains. Or so Alex had imagined, during a brief fragment of a dream, while sleeping on the slow night train to the capital.

PART II
GRAY CAPITAL IN WINTER

1

She suddenly remembered the opening lines of one of Eminescu's lesser-known poems. It was the one her father once read to her, just before bedtime, when she was a little girl. *Of all the many tall ships leaving the safety of the shores, how many would be crushed by the cruel waves or sunk by the cold winds?*

Dana had just finished watering her beautiful violets and ferns. The same types of violets and ferns she had given Alex on his birthday a few years earlier. Alone in her small, crowded apartment, she felt unbearably wistful. She remembered Alex's last visit, the day after she had failed her first entrance exam to medical school by a very slim margin. Only 0.2 percent. More than eleven thousand candidates, from all over the country, had competed for about a thousand positions. The results of the exams were cold-heartedly revealed, for all to gawk at, on long white sheets of paper taped to a stone wall, on the outer perimeter of the university courtyard. Dana's name ended up second below that dreaded red line, which separated the relatively few lucky new medical students from the many pretenders who had to wait for at least another year before trying again.

She had spent two years of her young life studying hard and taking expensive private lessons each lousy week, in organic chemistry, physics, physiology, and anatomy, in preparation for those dreaded exams. She had wasted two years for the privilege of seeing her name stuck on the wrong side of that cruel, arbitrary red border, less than a centimeter away from her goal. Would the nation have suffered greatly, if they had admitted one thousand and two new medical students that year?

The morning after the results of the exams had been posted, Alex came by unexpectedly to show his support and try to cheer her up. It seemed like a hopeless task. Dana and Alex had ended their relationship several weeks earlier, shortly after the high school prom, and Alex might have felt a bit guilty about the seemingly casual way in which he had simply walked away, without any coherent explanations. Although he was normally quite talkative and articulate, he did not have anything meaningful to say on the uncomfortable subject of their breakup, and he also carefully avoided that topic during his last brief visit.

Understandably, Dana felt too discouraged and distracted to act as a very good host. Besides, Alex was obviously in a hurry, although he made an effort not to show it. He was carrying an enormous backpack, and appeared to have stopped by on his way to the railway station. They were both aware of the awkwardness of the moment. Dana knew it would have been futile to pretend to be brave in front of Alex, under the circumstances. At the same time, she was too worn out to talk at length about her feelings and her hopes. Instead, she found it easier to indulge in a bit of well-earned and heartfelt self-pity.

"My plans for the future are obvious. I have another meaningless year to waste, mindlessly studying those useless textbooks, before I can fail the next idiotic entrance exam," she said. "If there is a purpose to my stupid life, I sure can't find it."

"Ah, but there is always a purpose, ma chère. You are too good a person to let a little thing like a temporarily failed career plan ruin your positive outlook on life. Even today, after you've just missed out on gaining acceptance into the ranks of the privileged, you still found the time, I presume, to feed your cat and water your plants. You've done a few small good deeds already, and it's only ten in the morning. I'm sure your cat knows very well that your life has at least one vital purpose," Alex replied, and his uncharacteristically kind remarks broke through Dana's sadness, for a moment, and made her smile. It was only a little smile, but it felt very good. Since the sudden separation, she had constantly tried to convince herself that Alex was much too self-centered and egotistical to be worth missing. But then his visit, however brief, managed to weaken considerably, and perhaps unfairly, the very foundations of that almost established conviction.

They had not really spoken to each other since Alex's short stopover. After that, they had only seen each other briefly at a few parties, or on the street, and had exchanged polite greetings, but nothing more, and Alex was in the company of a new girlfriend every time. His romantic relationships never seemed to last for very long. A few years had passed, her cat had died, and Dana was now well into her medical studies, earning top grades. Her father, the reputable surgeon, would have been very proud of her accomplishments.

On this typically gray winter day, she felt a compelling need to stay away from her classes, at the university. A lingering sadness had taken hold, deep within herself, preventing her from leaving the apartment. For that was the day of Alex's final departure.

A few more lines from the brief poem came into her mind. *Of all the migratory birds flying overseas, how many would be brought down by the high winds and drowned by the merciless waves?*

2

Alex was walking home one evening, when a dreaded light green Jeep of the Ministry of the Interior pulled right in front of him, blocking his way.

"Get in," barked one of the middle-aged officers in the car.

"Get lost," was Alex's cold, spontaneous reply.

"Get in, and stop wasting time. It's for your own good."

The Jeep sped along the dark empty boulevards on its way to the headquarters deep in the heart of the Old Town.

Alex was escorted directly to the sumptuous office of a regional director, whose inflated sense of self could be read in every feature of his fat face. The inevitable angry speech, full of words rendered meaningless, such as "betrayal," "duty," and "patriotism" followed, and Alex stood there, stone-faced, with unreadable eyes, wondering when the sweating idiot before him was finally going to get to the real point of the unexpected meeting. While he waited, Alex kept himself entertained by imagining such things as a truckload of assorted manure being dumped, again and again, on the high official's pumpkin-shaped head, and a giant mechanical boot repeatedly kicking the secret policeman's enormous behind.

Finally, after more than twenty unbearably tedious minutes, the speech started to wind down: "And don't think you'll have it made in your decadent new world, my young deserter. Oh no, not for a minute. You'll find out the truth, when you get there. Oh yes, oh yes… Unemployment, crime, poverty, slums, drugs, chaos, cults… Western agents trying to recruit you in shopping malls. Maybe that's what you're looking for. Maybe that's just what you want. Because otherwise you're in for some nasty surprises, young man. Oh yes you are. You mark my words. Remember my words when you'll be lying in the gutter somewhere feeling sorry for yourself. It didn't have to be this way. When I think of how our state provided you with everything: free education, free medical care, all kinds of opportunities.

We attended to your every whim, like attentive parents. And this is how you repay us. By running away in the middle of the night, like a thief! But it's too late now, oh yes, much, much too late. You're here to get your foolish wish, and I'm here to grant it. I'm here to repay your disloyalty to your homeland. It makes me sick to my stomach to do this. Sick, you understand? Oh yes, oh yes… I have feelings too, you know. It nauseates me. But I have a job to do. A job for the homeland. And it is not an easy job, you know. Of course, you wouldn't know, would you? How could you know about duty? About self-sacrifice and love of country… But I don't have any more time to waste on this sordid, sad affair. I already gave too much attention to the likes of you. You have exactly two seconds, *exactly* two seconds, to decide which type of passport you want. Pick the one with the blue covers, and you remain a citizen of the motherland. Take the one with the brown covers, and you give up your citizenship, and your rights. Don't say we didn't give you a choice. Well, I don't have all day, what's it going to be?"

"I'll take the brown one."

"Suit yourself. I'm disappointed, but not surprised. Sign these forms and then leave. You have exactly one week to make arrangements to cross the border, by land or by air."

And that was it. Almost anticlimactic. All of a sudden, the final weight was off Alex's shoulders, and the butterflies in his stomach started to come to life and flutter their wings, in anticipation of his upcoming long trip. The trip that was going to change every aspect of his life.

3

As Alex crossed the dark street, away from the dreaded headquarters building, a fairly old man — a happy drunk — approached him, and asked: "Excushe me, do you have a light?"

"I don't smoke," Alex responded.

"I don't shmoke either, shir. I jusht wanted a light," said the man, as his laughter deteriorated into a nasty sounding cough.

"You know, dear shir, I can remember a time when the shity wash lit sho well, you could shee a pin in the shtreet at night. A pin, shir, even a pin! But that wash before, in the old days… When I wash young."

Alex felt sympathy for the old man, but couldn't help wondering if this was some sort of a set-up — somebody trying to deliberately draw him into a risky conversation in a dangerous public place. He usually did not mind engaging in such discussions, but now he felt tired and had a passport to protect. Therefore, he simply said, "Perhaps this may not be the best place for these types of recollections," and he silently pointed at the imposing building behind them with his head.

"Ah, right you are, kind shir. Right, right, you are," said the old man, putting an unsteady upright index finger in front of his lips, to show that he understood the message.

4

Alone in the deserted city center, Alex finally decided to start walking home. The futile half-hour wait had convinced him that this would be one of those nights when the buses just wouldn't be coming. This realization came more as a relief than an annoyance because, despite his tiredness, Alex was actually looking forward to one last long solitary walk through his hometown. This had been the center of his world, and he knew he would need a very long time before he could regard any other city the same way.

It was a beautiful night — unusually mild for the season, and he felt privileged to be alone with his thoughts and memories. He needed this quiet time all for himself, without any constraints at all — not even the often-pleasant constraints imposed by the company of his friends.

Although he was perfectly capable of being the center of attention and the life of many a party, Alex was more comfortable on his own. That is when he did his best work and could think most clearly. Being sociable could be fun, in moderation, but it was always nice to be able to retreat to the refreshing shelter offered by solitude — a place where you never had to worry about being witty or charming or misunderstood.

Alex knew the downtown core and many other neighborhoods in the city of his birth very well, and could easily find his way around, even though he didn't actually know the names of many of the streets he was walking on. He had an excellent sense of direction and never needed to rely on a map, which was fortunate, because detailed maps of the capital were very difficult to find.

On his way towards a major boulevard, Alex passed by the venerable university building where his father had taught for many years. During the summer vacations of his childhood, Alex occasionally accompanied his father to the university, and sometimes, while waiting for his father in the office, he used to draw caricatures of various people he saw passing by in the corridor. The kind-hearted secretary in his father's academic department liked Alex's drawings, so he gave her one of them as a souvenir. The secretary was delighted and promised to frame it and place it on a wall in her office. Apparently, she had kept her promise, and Alex wondered if the drawing was still there, above the secretary's desk. Those were happy summer days, when he went with his father to the movies at the various theaters lining up the boulevard nearby, and afterwards, they would have lunch at a nice cafeteria located beside the newly built Intercontinental Hotel, which was by far the tallest building in the downtown area at that time. Alex's mother could not join them, because she worked at a research institute outside the city and had a long commute each work day. More than three years had passed since he had seen his parents, and he missed them.

He thought about the upcoming flight across the ocean and his fear of flying. The well-meaning advice he had received came back to him all at once. "Don't worry. Statistically, flying is the safest mode of transportation," Victor had said.

Really? Did they include leisurely rides on horse-drawn carriages in the analysis? If a bus breaks down before reaching its destination, you can usually walk away. Who cares about statistics when you're suspended in thin air at over ten thousand meters without a parachute or any control over your life? There is no safety net underneath, and nothing you can do if there is some type of mechanical failure or human-made error. Up there, one mishap can mean the end. In between take-off and landing, you can only get off by falling.

And this was going to be a long flight over frigid water. The North Atlantic in winter. No nearby airports or emergency crews, and plenty of time for something to go wrong. If the plane goes down and you somehow survive the crash landing, and your life-jacket — assuming you have time to put it on — keeps you afloat in the middle of the ocean, the sharks will probably find you well before the rescuers do, although hypothermia will most likely kill you first.

Not only do you have to pay the huge price of a ticket, but on top of that, you also lose the ability to govern your own life in any meaningful way for several hours. You surrender your fate to total strangers — people you have no reason to trust. You pay them handsomely, and, in return, they take away your peace of mind and independence. And all the while, they treat you like a helpless infant, patronizing you, telling you the weather is fine when you can see the dark clouds gathering, and deciding when and what to feed you and when they will let you unbuckle your seat belt so you can get up for a little while and move a bit to recover some semblance of feeling in your toes. And if you want even something as basic as a bit of extra water, you have to press a button and ask for help, like a feeble invalid. What a great freaking deal! What a unique opportunity to understand the real meaning of constant tension and unrelieved stress!

"Try to sleep, and you won't even notice the hours flying by," Dan had advised. Alex had wondered if that was meant as a joke. Was it a weak attempt at sarcasm? How can anyone possibly sleep under those kinds of circumstances?

In fact, you arrive at the airport already exhausted and cranky since it was impossible to sleep at all during the night before the flight. Although, as a passenger, you are completely at the mercy of the pilots and the elements, you just can't help listening for possible subtle changes in the sound of the airplane engines or wondering about any slight unusual movements of the aircraft. And sometimes those movements are not all that slight. Sometimes there is major turbulence, especially when you make the transition from land to sea and sea to land, or go over mountains, or, heaven forbid, fly through a storm.

Sometimes you have to watch out because, even though your seat belt is on, as it should be most of the time, the turbulence can make the food cart hit the ceiling and then come back down on your head. Flattened by a flying food cart while strapped to a chair — now that would be a glorious, headline-making way to go! Really spectacular. Would rank highly among the most idiotic and undignified ways to check out.

Still slightly better than having to endure the airline food, perhaps, or being trapped beside an overly talkative moron for all those hours — the type who introduces himself as soon as he sits down and then asks for your bun at mealtime. You're trying to hear if the engines are still running as they should and the fellow in the seat next to yours keeps going on and on about his painful bunions, his crazy aunt and her thirty cats, his collection of beer bottle caps, the likelihood of developing fatal blood clots during long flights, his hernia operation, or the time when a plane he was on was hit by lightning and he was the only survivor. And if you are lucky enough to land safely, after all that stress and turmoil, you'll likely get sick in the next few days anyway, since a lot of the air you breathe on the airplane is recirculated, which means the airborne germs any of the passengers may carry can easily become your germs.

Alex remembered his very first flight. It was one of his earliest memories. He was probably about three or four years old, and he had a high fever. He was vacationing with his parents at the seaside when he became ill, and his parents decided to fly back home immediately since the train ride would take too long. Alex had a clear recollection of trying to alert his fellow passengers that they were all going to the clouds, presumably to live there permanently, and he couldn't understand why nobody seemed to take his warnings seriously. What was wrong with all these people? How could they just sit there, doing nothing, and accept their fate? Alex did not want to move to the clouds, and he couldn't understand why anyone else would. He wanted to return home to his toys and his friends, and the safety of his room. But no one understood him. All in all, it had been a very unsettling and unpleasant experience, and his opinions on flying had not improved since then.

He was going to Canada, a country where he knew no one except for his parents, and although he always publicly projected an image of absolute certainty when it came to the overall net benefits of his upcoming departure, privately, he was fighting against some inevitable doubts and regrets. What would he do there, so far away from Europe and everything that was familiar to him? Would he succeed or fail spectacularly? Would his lofty dreams and youthful ambitions get swallowed up by bitter middle-aged mediocrity in a cold faraway land? Would he find peace of mind? Would he enjoy himself?

Would hockey — a very minor sport in his country — ever replace his beloved football, a sport not much in favor in North America? He used to love going to weekly football games with his father on Sundays — would that ever happen again? Alex was a fan of a smaller club from his father's hometown, in the northwestern part of the country, far away from the capital. This club struggled at times, and was often in danger of relegation to the second division. Its best players, like good players from a variety of other provincial clubs, were often taken by the two big teams in the capital — the army's team and the team supposedly representing the security services. Aside from having the top players and presumably access to more funds and better training facilities, these powerful teams in the capital often bene-fitted from favorable refereeing as well, which made the rare occasions when Alex's small club came to the capital and won a match even more remarkable and joyous. Like everything else in their country, football had also been contaminated by pol-itics and corruption. In the last few years, an obscure team from the president's village had risen to the top division by winning with highly improbable scores. It was unheard of for a village team to progress that far, but anything connected to the president was heavily promoted in those days, often to an absurd and almost comical degree.

Alex remembered a particularly outrageous episode when the obviously corrupt referee prolonged the match by ten full minutes, incredibly enough, and called a penalty against the opposition at the very end for a fictitious infraction to allow the army team, which was in a tight race for the title, to win. This had been such a blatant and brazen example of a phony result that even some of the usually com-pliant sports journalists expressed certain reservations in print. One of the articles listed fifteen reasons why the army team should not have won the match. It was a start. Now, if only commentators would dare to expand their criticisms to other issues as well there could be some faint hope on the horizon. But that was probably too much to expect, at least in the near future.

Watching that farcical contest reminded Alex of a story Gabriel once shared about his time in the army. The officers were playing the soldiers in a football match which went on for as long as it took to make sure the officers to would win. No other outcome was allowed. So, the game continued well past the regular time limit, until the tired and poorly fed soldiers finally got the point and conceded, only to watch the officers celebrate as if they had won the World Cup. As if the result was ever in doubt. The sergeant, who also acted as the referee, had made it clear to the new recruits from the beginning that winning against the officers would have dire consequences, such as additional long marches in the heat of the day, the cancellation of the next leave, and reduced food rations. Still, the soldiers played hard, including Gabriel, who normally didn't fancy the sport. The threats and the intimidation seemed to strengthen their resolve and embolden them. They fought like lions, but almost each time they scored, an absurd penalty would be called against them, and later on, a couple of their best players received a red card simply for mild and accidental contact with an opposing player in the field. And yet, when an officer viciously kicked a soldier during the game, the referee/sergeant simply laughed and told the injured soldier, who ended up with a broken leg, to pick himself up and act like a man for a change. With two players eliminated from the field and one badly injured, the soldiers finished the game with only eight men, against the eleven officers, and it still took nearly two and a half hours — almost an hour longer than a regular match — for the officers to prevail. It had been a sickening display of the arrogance of power, and Alex wondered how the officers, or the army team, which went on to win the league title that season, could possibly enjoy such undeserved results.

Still, the passion for football endured, and Alex knew he would miss the games, the heated discussions with other fans at the stadiums and elsewhere, and even the familiar taste of the roasted sunflower and pumpkin seeds available in large amounts during the matches. He suddenly found himself craving the excessive salt the roasted pumpkin seeds were sometimes coated with.

Football was the most important and accessible sport they had. Almost all the boys in his country played the game during their childhood and adolescence. It was easy to do. All you needed was an empty field, one ball, and a couple of rocks at each end — placed several meters apart and acting as substitutes for proper goalposts. There was no referee, so the kids would keep track of their own version of the rules of the game as well as they could. If there was enough time, they would play until one team scored twelve goals first. If not, they played until the one the ball belonged to had to go home. There was little strategy, and not much of a game plan, and usually almost all the players went forward at the same time, making defense a secondary concern, and the job of the goalkeeper the most unrewarding of all.

Alex and his mates had played in almost any conditions: on dirt, on concrete, in school yards, on quiet streets, and even in the school corridors during breaks between classes, when they sometimes used an eraser instead of a ball, stirring up a lot of dust trying to kick it (and often kicked each other's legs instead). During summer vacations in a small mountain town, he even played the game on a tilted field located on top of a steep hill, when the main challenge was running downhill to get the ball each time it went outside the playing area, which happened quite often.

He remembered the inhospitable football field behind his old high school. It had an odd, irregular shape, and was covered by cement, which made any fall during the game not just painful but also potentially dangerous. What kind of lunatic would decide that cement was a suitable surface for a football field, particularly on school grounds? At the start of the Physical Education class, the teacher simply gave the boys a ball and let them play football for an hour, which was much appreciated and a welcome relief from the stress of their many other courses. And sometimes, the opportunity to play would present itself during unexpected gaps in the schedule as well.

Alex recalled one such incident. They were wasting time as usual in the shop class when even the instructor — a short, chubby, and balding former factory worker (looking a bit like an overweight version of Louis de Funès) with a rudimentary education and a fiery temper — had enough and decided to send the students home early. Fearing repercussions from the principal in case this breach of protocol was discovered, the shop teacher told the boys to go straight home, as quietly as possible. So, naturally, Alex, Dan, and a few others headed straight for the football field at the back of the high school and started playing. They were in the middle of a pretty good game when they saw the irate and alarmingly red-faced shop teacher coming towards the field with a long wooden stick in his hand (yes, he was indeed that primitive). Alex and almost all his colleagues promptly took evasive action and climbed over the tall concrete wall around the schoolyard before the angry teacher could get to them, but Dan never made it over the wall on time and was caught. He somehow did not realize what was happening until it was too late, and then he simply froze. The teacher — if he could be called that — used a remarkable variety of swear words, threats, and demeaning expressions but did not hit anything other than air and the ground with his stupid stick. The next day, the entire group of students that had disobeyed the shop teacher's instructions was required to install barbed wire above the tall wall surrounding the high school, making future escape attempts even more challenging. Their school used to look somewhat like a fortress, and now it looked like a penitentiary. The only thing still missing was a moat.

Unlike the real football, followed avidly by most of the world, the North American sport with the same name was played mostly with the hands, rather than the feet, and was therefore obviously misnamed. Why did they do that over there? Couldn't they find another more appropriate, distinctive, and original name? Then again, the name handball was already taken. Helmet ball, perhaps?

Although he was interested in a variety of summer and winter sports, Alex was only very vaguely familiar with North American football and baseball, and did not know the rules of those games. North American football seemed somewhat like a more violent and less chaotic version of rugby, requiring substantial protective head gear and a lot of extra padding. Could he ever learn to really appreciate baseball? It seemed like a strange sport, where players spent a lot of time sitting around, which may explain why some of them had prominent bellies and did not look like professional athletes. Quite a few appeared to put more effort into chewing impressive amounts of tobacco than into running around the oddly shaped field. And the so-called "strike zone" was apparently a crucial but abstract notion, whose exact boundaries only existed in the mind of the umpire. And every year, the winning team of each baseball season was decided after something apparently called the *World Series*, even though only American teams took part. What on earth was going on over there? How exactly did they develop these weird games, and how many other strange things would be discovered on the continent adjacent to the northwestern side of the Atlantic?

It also appeared that the concept of relegation to lower divisions for the teams finishing at the bottom of the standings did not exist in major North American sports leagues. To Alex, this seemed like a significant shortcoming and an inexplicable failure, since the struggle to avoid relegation, each year, could be just as interesting as the competition for the title among the top teams. In European football leagues, relegated teams from superior divisions were replaced at the end of each season by newly promoted teams from lower divisions, and this allowed for yearly changes in the composition of the divisions, as well as giving many teams other meaningful and vital goals to strive for. In fact, first place was not a realistic objective for the vast majority of the teams, and trying to stay out of the danger zone that could lead to relegation added urgency and significance to matches which otherwise may have been almost meaningless, or played only for pride. But, apparently, in North American sports, they didn't believe in relegation. Only the title race mattered there. Otherwise, regardless of whether you finished second, in the middle of the standings, or dead last, you still had the same chance as everyone else to compete for the title the next season, and there was no cooling-off period in the lower divisions for the worst losers.

Alex wondered if his interest in sports would gradually wane in North America, and if not getting excited about baseball or North American football would isolate him somewhat from other fans over there and make him even more of an outsider on the continent destined to become his new home.

The unsettling questions kept on coming, racing through his active mind, as he focused on his upcoming departure. Would he ever be able to write in English at the level he had reached in his mother tongue? Would he have a foreign accent forever, while speaking English? Would it matter? Would he ever find friends better than the ones he was about to leave behind? And even if he did, those new friends could never know what he was like and what he went through when he was very young. They could never be childhood friends.

What did he really know about Canada? Very, very little, in fact. It was a vast country — the second largest in the world — with long winters, and colorful maple forests in the fall. Pierre Trudeau was the prime minister, and Ottawa was the capital — one of the coldest capital cities in the entire world. The official languages were English and French — fortunately, the very same foreign languages he was taught in school. What else? The Summer Olympics took place in Montreal in 1976, and Nadia won her gold medals and earned her top marks there. That was a good memory, but still not nearly enough to give him a strong impression of this distant land. Despite his excellent education and perfect memory, Alex couldn't think of a single Canadian writer, artist, or scientist. Someone told him that the members of the band Rush were actually Canadian, but he wasn't sure. He had assumed they were American. In any case, he couldn't think of a single Rush song. And in Canada, it was very likely that almost no one had heard anything about the writers, artists, or scientists of his homeland. His parents had sent him a guidebook with information about the new country he was hoping to move to, and some of the photographs looked nice, particularly the ones showing the Rockies, but those mountains were very far from the eastern part of the country where he was supposed to settle. Clearly, his total knowledge of Canada was still minuscule, and many Canadian secrets remained to be uncovered, including the correct pronunciation of intimidating words such as Saskatchewan. In a way, he felt as uncertain about life in Canada, as he had been about going to school on that first day of classes in grade one, when he was six years old. On that day, he had wondered how he would handle his new life as a student and whether he would do well or not, and that type of uncertainty was confronting him once again now, as he contemplated another plunge into the unknown.

He knew he couldn't express any doubts publicly, because the government officials in charge of his file were looking to use any possible hint of uncertainty on his part as an excuse to delay the processing of the required documents even further. Several officials had threatened him with everything from a long stint in the army to hard labor, but Alex did not take the threats all that seriously. He had assumed the main purpose had been intimidation. They were trying to convince him to give up, change his mind, denounce his parents, and withdraw his application. He could not give in, and had to remain steadfast in the pursuit of his main goals. Once you started a process like this, there could not be room for any second thoughts. Either they broke you or your determination broke them.

But there was another, less practical, reason for Alex's public show of certainty about his uncertain future. Truth be told, he enjoyed his status as an outsider, and the envy this generated among many of his friends and acquaintances. Even though there were many risks, and nobody could be sure what kind of future awaited him across the Atlantic, almost everyone he knew seemed to believe that he was really the luckiest person in the world. It was indeed good to make a new start and leave behind a damaged society where the general tension and unhappiness were growing and threatening to explode any day into long-anticipated open revolt.

Things were obviously getting worse and worse. There were longer and longer line-ups for less and less food — even sugar and cooking oil were being rationed. Power outages were more and more frequent. Warm water was becoming an unpredictable luxury and apartments had minimal or no heat during the winter. On top of all that, the tired people had to endure increasingly delusional presidential pronouncements and decrees, and official suggestions that everyone should consume fewer proteins and use only one weak light bulb per room. Pretty soon they may force the population to switch to candles and ban electricity altogether — a return to a medieval way of life. The more conspicuous police presence in the streets was meant to intimidate and suppress any possible protest against all these impositions.

As he walked by a shuttered grocery store, in the middle of the night, Alex could see a few senior citizens patiently waiting in line in front of the entrance already, even though the store would not open for many hours, and there was no guarantee any useful products would be available inside. Meat was particularly sought after, since it was becoming more and more scarce, but people became used to line up for pretty much anything. In fact, sometimes people joined long lines without even knowing exactly what items might be available. The assumption was when there was a line-up, there might be some hope to get something. Anything.

The touching and fleeting triumph of faint hope over miserable experience would be illustrated by a typical conversation between somebody who had just joined the line and the person in front of him: "Do you know what we're lining up for?"

"No idea, but judging by the size of this line, it has to be something good," would be the answer.

Often, there was nothing good, however, and sometimes, there was nothing at all, and some worried-looking store employee, possibly expecting a riot, would

come out and announce the delivery truck had not come that day, or the supply
had been rapidly exhausted.

And the worse the general situation became, the more intense the official propaganda turned out to be. No one ever mentioned food shortages and sharply declining standards of living on the TV news, of course. On the black-and-white
screen, everything was perfect. The only "regular" people interviewed on TV were
always unnaturally happy and peculiarly grateful to the government and the president for virtually every little thing in their seemingly great and worry-free lives.
There were never any clouds on their horizons. Occasionally, some of them would
even perform a little "spontaneous" folk dance in front of the cameras, thereby
proving beyond doubt they were deranged. TV announcers and "personalities"
were only there to feed disinformation to the masses under the watchful eyes of
the authorities. Not that anyone was taking the official news seriously anymore.

Aside from a handful of seemingly insane party activists, Alex did not recall
meeting anyone who truly believed the slogans and the blatant lies masquerading
as news. After roughly forty years of repeated failures and constant repression,
pretty much everyone knew their political system was broken and could not work.
And yet, due to fear and complacency, they all pretended to go along with the
official accounts, and chanted and clapped when told to, just so that they could at
least keep the little they still had and stay out of bigger trouble with the authorities.

For more reliable and intriguing information, people listened to the forbidden
Free Europe or BBC broadcasts on their portable radios. Because of the jamming
from their own government agencies, this information was sometimes difficult to
follow since it was often heard in disjointed fragments, but the people listened
carefully anyway, because they were eager to hear the truthful reports, which could
never appear in their country's government-controlled media. In a way, the jamming of these Western European broadcasts enhanced their popularity. Presumably, government officials in their country would not try so hard to block these
types of alternative news, if they didn't find them exceedingly embarrassing and
inconvenient.

Throughout the long and arduous process of applying for permission to leave
the country, Alex had been berated often by various cowards who took advantage

of their official positions, and the situation, to lecture him about the superiority of the (multilaterally developed) communist society and the inevitable rapid decline of the West. And yet, Alex could see that even these high-ranking officials did not believe in the corrupt system they were defending — the very system that had given them their lofty positions and undeserved perks. They were merely angry because they knew Alex would soon move beyond their control and join the ranks of free men in a less restrictive and more enjoyable and comfortable part of the world. The West may not have been perfect, but at least it looked like it could be more fun, overall.

Although he couldn't talk back under the circumstances, Alex would have liked to ask these bastards some simple questions: If the West was indeed declining sharply and communist societies were so much better in comparison, then why was there a one-way steady migration of people towards the supposedly bankrupt and decadent West? Why didn't we have long line-ups of disappointed Westerners desperately trying to get into communist countries instead? Why was it necessary to put up the Berlin Wall, and tall barbed wire fences around borders, and to jail or shoot would-be defectors, to keep people inside lands supposedly "blessed" by having governments which had embraced the Marxist-Leninist doctrine? Could anybody think of a single communist country, anywhere, in the entire history of the planet, which had been prosperous and democratic for any significant length of time? No, of course not. There were no such examples, and anyone who wasn't truly brainwashed or completely crazy knew it. People could not deny the truth of their own daily experiences, and the increasingly widening gap between the reality of their difficult lives and the bizarre fantasy delivered through the official propaganda was becoming more and more difficult to ignore.

Despite all this, recent estimates showed that their country's Communist Party had two or three million members — an astonishingly high percentage of the adult population. Privately, party members tended to complain just as much as everyone else about the worsening living conditions and the absurdity of daily life. But that evidently did not stop them from joining a party most regarded as the primary source of their problems. They said they did it to survive, advance their careers, and ensure they were well regarded at work and in society in general. It wasn't a big deal, they said — it's not like they had any decision-making powers, after all. It was just a way to get along and avoid being blacklisted. Alex always found these often-heard excuses and justifications pathetic, cowardly, and self-serving.

Neither his parents nor his grandparents had joined the party, despite repeated invitations and pressure to do so from various influential officials. The refusal to join, especially for a top intellectual, was a career-limiting move as well as a badge of honor, in some ways. You were regarded with suspicion in some circles and respected for your integrity by many at the same time. There were only a couple of other students in Alex's high school class whose parents were not party members. Everyone else's parents, including Dan's father and mother, joined without hesitation, and some even volunteered to give speeches in support of official policies and regulations, like the obedient pawns they had become.

When Alex was approached about possibly joining the party by some witless local activist, he declined by stating he wasn't worthy of the honor, since he liked to listen to Western rock music, and enjoyed a decadent lifestyle, and therefore he hadn't reached the elevated level of consciousness that would undoubtedly be expected, and likely even required, for a true believer in communism. The befuddled party official insisted, stating that such a level of "political maturity and understanding" could be achieved in time even by the most recalcitrant elements and that the first step was to acknowledge the error of one's ways, to which Alex had replied: "I am afraid I am a lost cause. Don't waste your time with me, when there are so many others who are much better candidates for recruitment. But if you ever want to discuss the error of your ways, I may be willing to listen."

Alex generally despised activists, and regarded them as shameless opportunists and mediocrities, who were using an exaggerated commitment to officially approved rigid ideology as a way to advance in life and elevate their social status, without having to work hard or become competent in any useful occupation. Most were relatively unintelligent busybodies who used activism to gain undeserved power over others. Activism was often a front meant to cover up the character flaws and intellectual inadequacies of deeply insecure and damaged cretins.

In the distance, in the middle of a major downtown boulevard, Alex could see a giant wooden arch, hastily put together for one of the many phony celebrations of non-existent national "triumphs" and the message on the arch advertised the supposedly "Golden Era" they were living through. It seemed like a sick joke. Quite subversive, actually.

It was as if someone was trying hard to make fun of the plight of regular people and dance on the graves where their hopes and dreams were now buried. A dangerous game — one the high officials were either too stupid or too arrogant, or both, to refrain from playing again and again. Just like the idiotic decision to stop broadcasting the overtime of a crucial international football match in order to show yet another mind-numbing presidential speech at some tractor factory, or something like that. Football was one of the few things a lot of people could still look forward to, and yet the morons at the top couldn't even leave that pastime alone.

It was like they were obsessed with finding new ways to annoy everybody. For example, a few years earlier, the publication of a genuinely interesting weekly magazine focusing on football had been suddenly stopped. There was no official explanation, of course, but apparently someone high up in government — possibly the top small man himself — decided the supposedly frivolous football magazine had to go, because — surprise, surprise — it had proven to be much more popular than the misleadingly-named *The Spark*, which was the dreadfully dull and virtually unreadable official newspaper of the Communist Party, also commonly known as the communist low-grade toilet paper. And no periodical could be allowed to be more popular than the official communist paper. So now, they were stuck with *The Spark*, which littered workplaces and park benches everywhere and lined plenty of birdcages, while the good football magazine many actually wanted to read was no more. There was no logical link between demand and supply. Only rigid, unwavering ideology. If people did not like what the Party provided, they had to be "re-educated" until they surrendered to the Party's whims.

It was not wise to keep poking the wounded bear. More and more people had less and less to lose. Their leaders' reckless stupidity was going to speed up the inevitable and much anticipated demise of the regime. But it wasn't just the national and regional leadership that was rotten to the core. According to persistent rumors, one in three adults in the country of his birth was an informer for the secret police. It was hard to trust anybody. The sticky tentacles of the suffocating security apparatus reached into every segment of society. There were informers, or potential informers, in every apartment building, every workplace, and even among his former high school and university colleagues. Alex sometimes wondered about the real motives of certain former colleagues he barely knew who seemed to have taken a serious interest in him for the first time only after they had found out he had formally requested to leave the country permanently. It wasn't easy to tell the difference between real dissidents and people hired to spy and entrap on behalf of the secret police. If you said too much to the wrong person you could be in serious trouble, and Alex was known to be dangerously outspoken at times. Whenever he became a bit nostalgic about his people and his land, he thought about all the informers and the other scoundrels, and renewed his confidence that he was doing the right thing by leaving this mess behind.

There were several giant holes in the ground in the Old Town, where vulnerable buildings destroyed by the massive earthquake once stood. And some of the architectural gems that had survived the earthquake were demolished anyway, or were about to be demolished, because of a dreaded and widely despised "urban renewal and restructuring" program whose main purpose was to eliminate as much of the legacy of the pre-communist past as possible and reshape the city according to the directives of the president and his accomplices and enablers. "The revenge of the morons," Alex muttered, as he looked at the dismal gaps all around. The beautiful theater building, where he attended his first play — Caragiale's *A Lost Letter* with his mother when he was nine years old — was gone already, as were several historic churches, a hospital built in the nineteenth century, and many venerable houses.

However, some familiar landmarks were still standing nearby — even the communists couldn't manage to destroy everything. His former high school was just around the corner. It was a more than three-hundred-year-old institution, and Alex realized he was about to move to a country much younger than his high school. Oh well, there's a lot of history still to be made over there, and I'll be part of it, he thought.

His last visit to his old high school, which had taken place quite some time after his graduation, had not been a pleasant one. He was putting together his voluminous file, containing all the documents necessary for the application to emigrate, and he needed a standard letter stating that he had indeed graduated. This should have been a formality — in fact, Alex had earned maximum marks in all of his graduation exams and already had his diploma — but, for some reason, the principal, a man who knew Alex quite well, refused to write the letter, presumably because he was afraid of the possible consequences. That is remarkably cowardly, even by local standards, Alex thought as he left the high school building for the very last time. Eventually, a letter with the required information did come by mail, many months later, but it was unsigned.

After high school, Alex wrote the university entrance exams without feeling much pressure to succeed. He was hoping to be allowed to leave his old country as soon as possible, of course, but thought that by becoming a local university student, however briefly, he would avoid possible menial jobs that might have been imposed on him otherwise. Without trying very hard, he still earned the top marks in the exams and was therefore placed first on the lengthy list containing the names of all the candidates competing for admission. He was allowed to pursue his university studies until he made his formal application to emigrate and forwarded the complete required documentation to the authorities. Afterwards, he was promptly kicked out of university, even though he was consistently the top student in all his courses and had done nothing to warrant such punishment. Apparently, the application to emigrate had been a serious enough offence by itself. Alex knew he would have to interrupt his studies in any event, and he was not surprised by the unfair decision, although he couldn't entirely disguise his disgust for the public way in which this was done (an announcement in front of the entire student body at a general assembly meeting).

The dean — who had gone to university with Alex's parents and had known Alex for many years — refused to meet with him to explain the decision, and made a show of theatrically crossing the street when he saw Alex coming. Of course, as a member of the Central Committee of the Communist Party, the dean had a lot to protect, and really did not have to do much in that role, except for mouthing embarrassing platitudes at regular intervals, and thanking the country's president constantly in the most exaggerated and servile ways possible for pretty much everything under the sun. "Thank you for your most magnificent and benevolent leadership, beloved and revered Comrade President! Supreme hero, your nation is eternally grateful to you! Without your unparalleled and inspiring guidance, we would all surely be lost, for you are the wisest of the wise, the bravest of the brave, the essence of all that is great in our superlative land..." — it was all quite nauseating indeed. Come to think of it, it couldn't have been that easy to crawl through life without any semblance of a spine and any trace of self-respect, at least, not at first, and not until numbness took over and completely replaced all pride. Nevertheless, there was talk that the dean was being seriously considered as the next Minister of Education, so spinelessness and lack of self-respect could pay off handsomely in their land. The things one had to do for access to a limousine and a title...

Alex was not particularly upset by his abrupt dismissal from the university, since it was sometimes difficult to concentrate on pursuing a degree he knew he likely wouldn't get a chance to complete, and he was keenly aware that he was essentially just killing time while waiting for permission to leave the country. Besides, having to put his university studies on hold due to his application to emigrate meant he had more time for his writing. His studies would resume, possibly at the University of Toronto, or McGill — he was going to sort all that out once he reached Canada — but for now, he had to prepare himself for his trip and tie as many loose ends as possible.

Pursuing an academic career in biology, which was one of his main goals, would have been nearly impossible in his homeland, in any case. In those days, in their country, if you could get yourself admitted to university and were interested in the life sciences, your best bet would be a career either as a doctor or a school teacher. Both were respectable professions, of course, but Alex wanted more — he was going to be a university professor, and conduct his own research and teach his own courses, without having anyone tell him what to do, or how to do what he did.

No one could stand in his way, certainly not the cowardly high school principal or the corrupt university dean.

He had lived with the idea of leaving his country permanently ever since his early teens, and this hadn't been an easy burden to bear. It was difficult to put down roots and settle down in a place you knew you would have to leave on a moment's notice. And it was hard to contemplate the more distant future when you had so little control over the timing and the nature of what would happen next in your life. He felt as if he had been living in a giant waiting room for too long. His parents had discussed their plans with him, in hushed tones, and sought his approval, but it was never clear if their dreams could ever become real. Tourist visas for trips to Western countries were always exceptionally difficult to obtain, and the restrictions on travel had become much more severe in the last few years.

At first, his parents had been reluctant to abandon their homeland, even when they had the opportunity to do so. In the early 1970s, for example, Alex and his mother had been allowed to travel to England for a two-week stay to join his father, who had been there for a year on a prestigious international fellowship. At the time, the entire extended family was convinced they would never return, which is why so many relatives came to the railway station to say goodbye. The long trip across Europe had been an eye opener, and even though he could not speak a word of English, or any other language except his mother tongue, Alex felt at home in the foreign lands and greatly enjoyed the experience.

Vienna was the first Western city he ever set foot in. They were changing trains there, and had a seven-hour stopover, which was enough to allow for a brief visit to some of the main landmarks. As he was enjoying a chocolate-coated marzipan bar while sitting in a spectacular candy shop near St. Stephen's Cathedral, ten-year-old Alex decided life was good and the West was indeed living up to his high expectations. The atmosphere seemed more relaxed than in his hometown, and there were considerably fewer policemen in the streets.

After that, the train ride continued through West Germany, along the scenic Rhine Valley, with medieval castles on top of green hills covered with vineyards, where everything seemed so perfectly neat and tidy, just like in the illustrations normally found in a book of classic fairy tales. Belgium was next, and the mainland portion of the train trip finally came to an end in the port city of Ostende. From there, the journey continued across the North Sea, on a massive ship, to Dover — the entry point into England. Alex's memories of England were somewhat scattered, since he had only been there for a relatively short period of time more than a decade earlier, and he'd had a very busy schedule, which included visits to many museums and other landmarks in several cities. For some reason, the one exhibit he remembered most vividly from his visit to the famous British Museum was the mummy of a cat. He insisted on seeing the statue of Peter Pan in London's Kensington Gardens, because he had read J. M. Barrie's beloved book, and had seen a photograph of the statue on the cover. In Liverpool, there was apparently a statue of the Beatles, but he did not see it during his brief visit there. At the time, he did not yet know much, if anything, about the Beatles anyway. He was amazed at the size and contents of the English breakfast, which consisted of heavy items such as sausage, bacon, and eggs, and made one feel sluggish from the very beginning of the day. Among his lasting recollections from the trip was the moment when he put a small coin into a slot machine for the first time and won many bigger coins in return. He then used the newly acquired loot to buy several colorful comic books, and even though he couldn't understand the captions, he enjoyed looking at the drawings and thought he could figure out the plot in most cases anyway.

A couple of years after Alex and his parents returned from England, they were visited at home by a publisher from the West — a middle-aged German man working for a prestigious American academic publishing company, who was there to discuss the publication of one of his father's scientific books. At the time, Alex was in grade six, and he had just started English lessons in school. Therefore, he was too shy to participate in the conversation, and felt he couldn't do so from a practical standpoint anyway since his English vocabulary was much too limited. His only contributions to the discussion in English with the publisher had been the word "fish" while pointing to the large aquarium in his room, and the formal introduction: "My name is Alex," which he managed flawlessly as his parents looked on with evident pride.

The more advanced English lessons would come a bit later. And the interest in the music of the Beatles and all sorts of American and British movies and TV shows certainly helped enrich the vocabulary, as well. "Learning English with John Lennon," Alex used to joke, as he got together with his friends to tape more songs and learn more lyrics. Some words and expressions were a little more challenging, of course, but Alex was not easily discouraged. For instance, while listening to Beatles songs, it took him some time to understand what a *Paperback Writer* was (the word "paperback" had been a difficult mystery to solve), or what *A Hard Day's Night* really meant, and trying to make sense of the lyrics of *I Am the Walrus* or *Come Together* proved impossible. Nevertheless, he enjoyed the music. He remembered the first time he heard *Eleanor Rigby*. He was attending a play about a DJ who played Beatles records. As soon as the song started, Alex was mesmerized, and couldn't think of anything else. He was surrounded by the amazing sound and deeply moved by the hauntingly beautiful melody and the devastatingly sad tale of loneliness and quiet despair. A touch of genius encapsulated in a song barely longer than two minutes. Two minutes Alex knew he was going to remember for the rest of his life.

All foreign movies shown in local theaters or on TV had subtitles, so he was used to reading the lines in his own language while also listening to the real voices of the original actors. This obviously required a literate audience, and was appreciated. For instance, dubbing and having John Wayne's voice replaced by that of a squeaky-voiced local actor would have ruined the movie.

However, one time, Alex faced a real test when Dan came up with a couple of free special tickets to a movie night at the American library in the capital. This was an unusual perk, and Alex was grateful to be invited to attend. The movie was *Saturday Night Fever*, which was not shown in regular theaters in their country. Given the circumstances and the setting, for the first time, Alex was viewing a foreign film without subtitles, and had to follow the dialogue of the young uneducated New Yorkers without the help of the translated written words at the bottom of the screen. This wasn't always easy, and Alex noticed that some of the other guests seemed to have similar problems understanding the slang and figuring out everything the fast-talking actors said. Nobody wanted to admit they were not up to the challenge, of course, so sometimes, if a member of the small audience laughed at some supposedly funny bit in the movie, others might follow and giggle as well, just to show they also understood the joke, even though they probably didn't. Dan kept watching an American official who had organized the event, and tried to copy his reactions. All in all, it had been an interesting evening, although Alex found the movie unexpectedly gritty. Having already heard the soundtrack on a record, he thought he was going to see some type of lightweight modern musical, but instead was exposed to the largely unhappy lives of a bunch of not-very-bright nobodies going nowhere in a rough part of New York. He also kept waiting for the Bee Gees to show up on the screen and was disappointed when he realized that wouldn't happen. Even though this was not always the ideal way to learn, movies and shows in English proved very valuable in helping Alex under-stand how more or less regular people spoke in America.

English classes in high school were not nearly as much fun. Their teacher was a rigid, vindictive, joyless, desiccated old prune who managed to suck the fun out of an interesting subject. She never forgave Alex and Dan for going to the movies once instead of attending one of her uninspiring lectures. She ran into them down-town, as she was walking towards the high school and they were walking towards the movie theater. Alex could have pointed out that the movie they were planning to see was British, but he thought better of it. He could have also explained that their high school was like a prison, with barbed wire on the back fence, so it was just as dangerous to try to get back in after managing to get out, but the teacher probably wouldn't have understood or cared. After that, she did her best to make their lives as miserable as possible.

Alex gave an excellent presentation in English in one of the classes, but all the teacher could say afterwards was: "You should not pronounce 'can't' like the Amer-icans." In other words, she objected to "can't" being pronounced more like "Kent" (the brand of foreign cigarettes which were the preferred currency for many bribes in their country at the time), as opposed to "Kant" (the German philosopher). Alex responded by stating that, at best, the English spoken in that class sounded more American than English anyway, since nobody there had British accents, and the teacher hated him even more afterwards.

In preparation for his imminent departure, Alex was taking private English lessons with Aunt Millie — a very nice old lady who was not a relative at all, of course, but just enjoyed being called that way. Aunt Millie was actually English — possibly the only English woman living in their country at the time, outside the British embassy. She had come to their land before the war for some unclear reason, fell in love with a local man, married him, and decided to stay. She was born in a free country, but spent most of her adult life behind the Iron Curtain because of love. Alex found that hard to understand. He grasped the idealistic and romantic side of the story, naturally, but couldn't fathom why that side was allowed to prevail over reason and common sense. Now, in her old age, Aunt Millie lived with her ailing husband in a small apartment near the railway station, trying to supplement her meager pension by giving private English lessons. Alex was her best student, and in recognition of that fact, she gave him a few books by Charles Dickens as a gift.

Leaving Dana should have been harder, perhaps, but had to be done in any event. Alex knew Dana would probably not agree to leave their country permanently, and even if she did, for his sake, he felt he was much too young and unprepared for that type of long-term, possibly lifelong, commitment to someone else. The only way he could have taken Dana to Canada legally was by marrying her, and marriage scared Alex perhaps even more than flying. His life was just beginning, and he was eager to experience much more, start new chapters and adventures, and dedicate himself to his work. Dana deserved true happiness with someone in a better position to help her find it.

Perhaps he was incurably selfish and self-centered and should have felt guiltier about it, but he simply couldn't. He knew he would really miss her for quite some time, but that was part of the price he had to pay for his freedom. It is always easier to have a relationship with someone you like rather than love. Who needs that kind of almost constant turmoil in one's personal life? It's not easy to feel continuously tested and evaluated. Alex was ready to just have some fun and enjoy life for a while, without any strings attached, without any deep commitments and responsibilities, and without having to carefully monitor everything he said in public, or to the person he was in a relationship with.

He remembered when Dana insisted on taking him to the ballet against his will. "You'll like it," she said, but he really didn't. In fact, as he had expected, he hated it, but couldn't quite say so, and was uncomfortable that entire evening, trying to pretend to appreciate a performance he thought of as silly and utterly pointless. It seemed ridiculous to leave somebody because of disagreements over the ballet, or opera (which Dana also enjoyed while Alex didn't), but there were several of these irritants, and Alex took these as signs that perhaps he didn't have that much in common with Dana (who also, inexcusably, did not appreciate football) and, therefore, they were not an ideal match. He wanted to be with someone in whose company he could feel more relaxed and comfortable, but he wasn't sure such a person existed, and he was in no particular hurry to settle down. He had always felt most comfortable in his own company and did not mind solitude one bit. Neither Dana nor Alex had any siblings, but Dana always wished she had one, whereas Alex was very happy to be an only child.

"Can you imagine having another one just like me around? The world wouldn't survive it," he once said with a mischievous smile.

Dana loved reading poems, and when she asked him if he ever wrote any, Alex jokingly responded: "I don't think I can write poetry. I am not that sensitive." The joke did not go over well. Besides, Alex wasn't being quite truthful. He had written a few poems — mostly bittersweet, satirical ones — but hadn't shown them to anyone. He wished Dana, and all his good friends, nothing but the best, but he also knew he had to look forward and chart a new course. His future would unfold elsewhere.

5

Gabriel met Anna at the seaside resort. He was playing piano in a summer band, gathered together to perform for the customers at a local restaurant during the peak of the tourist season. She had arrived in his country for the first time with a Scandinavian tour group, attracted by the cheap hotel prices and eager to experience something new. The resorts were open to both foreigners and locals, but the Western tourists stayed at separate hotels and could spend their foreign currency in special shops, where Gabriel and his compatriots were not allowed. These shops had products normally unavailable in the regular stores of their country, and Gabriel had sometimes found himself looking at the fancy display windows, wondering what Danish beer or Austrian marzipan might taste like. Gabriel was well aware that if he entered one of those shops and tried to make a purchase, he could have been arrested since the products found there could only be bought with Western foreign currency, and owning such currency was illegal for citizens of his country.

The band was usually playing a selection of bland old standards, but Gabriel sometimes stayed behind, after the other musicians wrapped up their regular daily set, to perform some music he truly enjoyed. On this occasion, he had just played an eclectic mix of compositions by Beethoven, Schubert, Lennon, McCartney, and Chopin, with some of his own added variations and arrangements, and was getting ready to leave the podium, when Anna stepped forward to compliment him on his wonderful performance. She was breathtakingly beautiful and natural, with a wonderful, broad smile and her long golden hair tied up in a bouncy ponytail, and she looked a bit like a young Agnetha Fältskog in the singer's early days with ABBA. Gabriel felt embarrassed by his heavily accented English, but he understood this foreign language much better than he was able to speak it, and he was moved by

Anna's kind words, and awestruck by her remarkable beauty. He couldn't quite believe someone so attractive would be interested in him.

"I wish I could play as beautifully as you," she said, and he promised to teach her.

6

As Alex kept walking on his journey home, he suddenly realized that he was passing by the park where his father had first taught him how to play tennis, over a decade ago. The tennis courts were still there in the middle of the park, but he couldn't see them clearly in the dark, through the chain link fence and all the vegetation. He enjoyed the game and felt a tinge of nostalgia while thinking about those old public courts, with holes in the nets and cracks in the playing surfaces, and wished he could have had just one more match there for old times' sake.

A few years after his first tennis lessons, at the beginning of high school, he had returned to the park with his class on a very hot summer day to plant trees. Dan was there as well. They had to attend school six days per week, for many hours. Even on Sundays — their only days off — they were sometimes summoned to perform "patriotic" duties and "voluntary" work in various places in and around the city. Occasionally, they were sent to plant crops in rural areas near the capital, or work on construction sites where they were not needed, but this time tree plant-ing in a city park was the task of the day. The activity seemed straightforward enough, but the work must have taken too long, and the sun must have been too powerful, because Alex started feeling unwell. It was a strange affliction — he was seeing everything in shades of blue and green, his fingertips felt numb, and he had problems controlling his speech, particularly when it came to the exact order of his words. In the bus on his way home, he was trying to talk to a worried-looking Dan, who lived in the same part of town, without much success. Alex remembered having to make a big effort and mobilize all his remaining intellectual resources to get the words out properly. He really had to struggle to say "See you later" at the end instead of "Later you see" or "You later see" or whatever other bit of nonsense. Alex staggered home from the bus station and was very ill, with a high fever, for a day or two afterwards. The diagnosis had been sunstroke. Alex was fair-skinned and, therefore, quite sensitive to the effects of the sun's merciless summer rays, and he did not take heat well. He used to joke that the sun did not like him, and the feeling was mutual.

But there were other memories tying him to the park, as well. This was the place where he had invited Dana to join him for their first walk together, on what turned out to be their very first date. The park was chosen simply because it was located not far from their high school, and was therefore easy to reach after the end of classes. Besides, it was a fairly private place — almost always nearly empty. They had walked in relative silence at first, about a yard apart, but by the time they left the park, a few hours later, they felt comfortable enough to hold hands, briefly, at least until they reached the crowded main street nearby. Dana was shy, cautious, sensitive, and thoughtful, and Alex felt sure there would be more dates to come.

They returned to the park again and again, and talked about everything, including Alex's plans to leave the country for good one day. Before his parents decided not to return from their Western trip to a scientific conference, Alex had only mentioned his desire to emigrate to three people outside his immediate family — Gabriel, Dana, and Victor — and all of them had to promise they would never divulge that potentially dangerous secret to anyone. As far as Alex could tell, they were all true to their word. Dana was understandably troubled by the news, especially because she felt that Alex, despite his general reassuring statements, was looking towards a future that did not necessarily include her. After a fairly long period of assessment and sometimes painful uncertainty, she was beginning to trust Alex more and more, and becoming more comfortable with the idea that they would be together for the foreseeable future. But, deep down, she had been afraid all along that her moments of intense happiness with Alex were too good to be real and couldn't last. From the very start of their relationship, she had to fight against the unsettling feeling that Alex was the type of person who could make a big initial impression, break down her defenses, and then one day vanish from her life, like a beautiful dream you could not hang on to for very long as you are beginning to wake up.

At that time, they had agreed to continue seeing each other, and she promised to stand by him and support any decision he would make on his future (secretly hoping that he would love her enough to stay or invite her to come with him). However, she sensed that he would eventually move on, and dreaded the idea that she would have to do the same at some point.

Alex had heard rumors that the park would be replaced by some giant official building, with construction set to begin in the very near future. Apparently, this was all a part of the reckless on-going plan to raze a large section of the old city center, including many irreplaceable historic buildings. It was becoming increasingly hard to believe that the capital had once been known as "Little Paris." Much of the elegant nearby district, known for its beautiful, patrician homes and small, quiet streets lined with mature linden trees, was already scheduled for demolition. Alex's grandfather's house was located in the middle of that district. It seemed very likely the house would not be spared, and the arrival of the eviction notice was probably only weeks away.

The affected area also included a major stadium where Alex had attended many football matches over the years. On one occasion, Alex even had the opportunity to enter the stadium not as a spectator, but as an active participant in the festivities taking place on the grass field itself. Hundreds, or perhaps even thousands, of school children had been recruited as extras for some sort of giant show meant to celebrate the leadership of the country's ruler. Alex, Gabriel, and many other kids from their elementary school were asked to form the president's name with their bodies, over the entire length of the football field. Alex observed privately that so many of them had to be inconvenienced, because the president's last name was so unusually long — if it would have been a shorter one (a four- or five-letter word, for instance), half of the school children could have stayed home.

Alex thought about the futility of it all. All the trees he had planted years ago, while developing sunstroke, together with the entire park, and the surrounding neighborhood would soon be obliterated and replaced by bare, scarred ground. And later on, intimidating neo-Stalinist architectural monstrosities — all massive concrete and right angles — would rise on this ground, and diminish this area, the way similar buildings had already contributed to the aesthetic degradation of so much of the rest of the city.

And this outrage was not restricted to the capital. There was talk that many traditional villages were going to be bulldozed and replaced by hideous and very basic concrete apartment blocks, supposedly in order to increase the total surface area of arable land in the countryside. Of course, the food shortages were due mainly to staggering incompetence and corruption, and an almost total misman-agement of the economy, as well as an obsession with paying the national debt as quickly as possible, and had nothing to do with the available arable land. But that didn't really matter. Economic forecasts were based on lies and wishful thinking. And the elimination of historic villages did not seem to give the rulers pause either. Communists always wanted to replace, and even erase, many old traditions and ways of life and create the utopian new society they always dreamed of, where all buildings looked the same and all the people shared the same party-approved thoughts. Complete uniformity and total conformity were the ultimate goals.

There was never any sound plan. Everything always started and ended with mindless ideology, and the whims of a severely undereducated dictator — an ele-mentary school drop-out — around whom obedient servants were building an unprecedented (by local standards) personality cult.

Alex remembered the mandatory high school visits to construction sites. They were sent there — a bunch of fifteen- and sixteen-year-olds — during what was supposed to be a part of their summer vacation, to help out the workers. There was never any training, and no safety gear was ever provided. None seemed avail-able, in any case. Live electrical wires were lying about, rusty nails were protruding, and all-around heavy blocks of concrete were being lifted by various cranes. A white dust enveloped everything, and you could feel it sink into your lungs and settle there. The entire scene seemed hazardous and chaotic. The foreman had not been informed high school students would be coming that day, and did not know what to do with them.

"Are you sure you're supposed to be here, and not over there?" he asked them, while pointing to another apartment building under construction across the road.

"This is where we were sent," said Alex.

And so, on the first day, the foreman instructed them to move a whole bunch of bricks from one side of the construction site to another, and then back again.

On the second day, the plan became more elaborate and diabolical. This time, each student had to carry one hundred bricks, ten at a time, from the ground floor to the tenth floor of an unfinished apartment building. The students had to also carry a piece of paper and collect twenty signatures, overall. One signature would be received from the foreman, each time a student left the ground floor with the bricks, and another signature would be given by a worker waiting on the tenth floor, when the student delivered the ten bricks there. There was no working elevator, so the students had to climb the stairs, holding the large, heavy bricks, each time, and then come down the stairs afterwards to pick up the next set of bricks and the next signature. It was hard and seemingly pointless work, and Alex came up with a bold plan to shorten the length of the torturous assignment, and enlisted Dan's help to achieve his goal.

All they needed were the twenty signatures in return for one hundred bricks delivered by each student. They didn't necessarily have to climb the stairs to the tenth floor ten times. Perhaps they could deliver all the bricks together, in one attempt. It would be difficult, of course, but it would significantly shorten their work day. Alex had spotted some type of large wooden stretcher, which looked sturdy enough to take the weight, and, together with Dan, he somehow piled two hundred bricks — the total load required for both of them — on there. The stretcher was almost unbearably heavy, but they each grabbed one end of it — Alex went to the front, and Dan to the rear — and made their way unsteadily up the stairs.

"I would rather take hernia over prolonged forced labor," said Alex.

Unfortunately, as they reached the ninth floor, after an agonizing climb, Dan stumbled on a loose cable, stretched out across the staircase, and dropped his end of the stretcher. All the bricks hit the floor and broke into pieces. Since the bricks had to be delivered intact, their big effort was in vain. It was a heartbreaking, not to mention backbreaking, setback.

"It's amazing," said Dan. "You would think at least one brick out of two hundred would remain intact."

"Nice to know they use this garbage for our apartment buildings," said Alex. "On the bright side, I suppose this also means these eyesores won't be standing for very long."

A few years later, Alex saw the foreman from the construction site again, while standing in line in front of the office where he had to submit his application to emigrate. The foreman did not remember him, of course, but seemed quite friendly and eager to talk.

"Relatives in the West?" the foreman asked.

"Parents in Canada," Alex replied.

"Lucky. I have a sister in Germany. Not sure if that counts as much, but I had to try, even if I may not leave this place until I'm eighty," said the middle-aged foreman with a smile.

7

When Dan saw Dana for the first time, he instantly thought she was the most attractive girl in the world, or, at the very least, the most attractive girl he had ever seen. She was tall, elegant, and slim, with beautiful light-brown wavy hair and captivating hazel-green eyes, and always moved about so gracefully, like a delicate dancer. And when he heard her pleasant voice, and the thoughtful, articulate comments she often made, he liked her even more. He was not the only one to appreciate Dana's great beauty. "Did you see her?" some of the other boys in the class whispered to each other, while looking admiringly at Dana on that very first day of high school. And the cruel Physics teacher — a bitter, damaged old man who only smiled when he failed a student, and never got close to anyone else — seemed to enjoy putting his hands on Dana's shoulders as he slowly turned her around towards the blackboard during unusually gentle examinations. Quite a few high school boys, including older ones from higher grades, were interested in courting Dana, and attempted to do so. Some brought her flowers, some wrote corny romantic poems, and a desperate one even tried a serenade, even though he couldn't really sing.

But Dana was naturally attracted to Alex, and the two of them formed a quick friendship and then started dating shortly after. By the end of the second year of high school, they always went to various parties as a couple, and they seemed happy together and impossible to break apart.

Dan understood — he felt he had no other choice, and tried to move on. Alex was his friend, and Dana was now Alex's girlfriend. Dan did his best to act supportive and magnanimous towards both of them. He thought this would be the honorable thing to do, and had nothing but positive things to say about Alex in Dana's presence.

He played the part of the loyal friend — a role he thought he was well suited for — perfectly, and, on one occasion, he even acted as the driver during the winter time, when Alex and Dana went to the woods on the outskirts of the city, and tied their sleigh to Dan's car. He was careful not to drive too fast, on the treacherous dirt road, as he was pulling his friends gently through the snow. It was a fun day, and they were all in great spirits afterwards, as they enjoyed a good dinner together at the capital's only Chinese restaurant.

Being the perennial nice guy and odd man out wasn't always easy for Dan, of course, and attending some of those high school parties with his friends became particularly hard for a while. After the food, the drinks, the jokes, and the livelier music, as the late evenings turned into nights, the lights would be dimmed and the softer songs would predominate. There would be little conversation, as couples would dance, slowly and closely together, to the sounds of the Bee Gees' *How Deep Is Your Love*, or Leo Sayer's *When I Need You* — the types of songs that seemed to set the appropriate mood for everyone but Dan. He often became quiet and melancholy as he watched Dana and Alex together on the dance floor, and usually found a reason to leave early.

Eventually, Dan learned to accept his predicament, or so he thought. He started to bring his own dates to the parties, and tried to think of Dana as a beautiful friend and nothing more.

However, after Alex left Dana, at the end of high school, Dan saw an opportunity to finally act on the feelings he had long tried to suppress. He couldn't do it right away, of course — Dana was going to need some time, and a general sense of decorum and propriety had to be maintained.

Still, he brought her flowers on her birthday — not just any flowers, but a gorgeous custom-made bouquet from the flower market — and was always there to offer support and understanding during her period of transition.

When Alex's parents failed to return from the West after a trip to an international scientific conference and it became obvious Alex would eventually apply for permission to join his parents in Canada, Dan had mixed feelings. On one hand, he knew he was going to miss his friend, but, on the other hand, Alex's upcoming departure also made it easier to contemplate a relationship with Dana. Dan thought highly of his friend, but always felt a bit overshadowed by him. With Alex about to leave the country for good, Dan thought he might have a better chance to impress Dana, and convince her they could be happy together. After all, they had been friends and high school colleagues, in the same class for four years, and now they were about to attend medical school together, and would have professional interests in common, as well. Dana's decision to pursue a career in medicine was important in convincing Dan to do the same.

Dan's parents were prominent MDs, and he had often heard them say that doctors should always marry other doctors, because no one else would understand them. Dan didn't necessarily believe that, and his parents did not seem to get along all that well. In fact, that "doctors should marry doctors" slogan was one of the very few things his parents ever agreed on. It was as if they were still trying to justify, after all those years of marriage, their misguided decision to get together. "We really can't stand each other, but at least we're both doctors," might have been another way of putting it.

Nevertheless, despite the questionable logic behind that silly slogan, Dan thought it would still be a useful thing to mention to Dana, at the right time, just to see how she felt about that type of statement. And if she disagreed, Dan could always try to pretend that he meant it as a joke, just to show how rigid his parents really were. Or he could say that some doctors could make ideal couples, and leave it at that. Besides, Dana knew all about growing up as the child of a doctor. Her father had been a well-respected physician as well, and their parents had known each other on a professional level well before Dana and Dan first met. But Dana never talked about her father, even though she kept his framed photograph on her living room wall.

8

"I grew up by the sea," Anna told Gabriel as they walked barefoot on the empty beach in the evening. "I live in a small house on a big hill, in Bergen. Have you ever heard of my hometown?"

"Edvard Grieg was born there. And that is also where he died," said Gabriel.

"Yes, indeed!" said Anna excitedly. "Perhaps one day you can be a famous composer and concert pianist, just like he was."

"I am far from that now," Gabriel replied, looking away from her and towards the incoming, white-crested waves.

"You have a special talent, and I love to hear you play. We have a piano in our living room, at home. Maybe you can also practice there, if you like," said Anna.

"You are very beautiful," said Gabriel, and, as he turned towards her, she pulled him closer, and then they kissed for the first time.

9

Alex, Victor, and Dan grew up in the same neighborhood in the west end of the capital, and attended the same prestigious high school — possibly the country's best — in the city center.

As a consequence of yet another round of reforms to the education system, most high schools became so-called "industrial" ones, presumably getting students ready for factory work. After the completion of the eight mandatory elementary school years, young people with university aspirations would have been wise to get into the relatively few remaining elite high schools where the focus was still mainly on intellectual pursuits. The competition for the limited number of available spots in these top high schools was predictably intense, and every year there were tough entrance exams which could, to an extent, decide the long-term academic futures of fourteen- and fifteen-year-olds. And then, after the first two years, at the end of grade ten, another crucial exam — the so-called Step Two exam — had to be passed, to allow students to stay in the high school of their choice. All this, of course, was in addition to the numerous other oral and written examinations they were subjected to, on a regular basis, in their many courses.

Most of the privileged and academically gifted students attending such "intellectual" high schools were enrolled in the mathematics and physics stream, which usually prepared them for a career in engineering (this had been Victor's choice). Aggressive industrialization was taking place in what had been until the last few decades largely an agrarian country, and all those new factories needed to be filled with workers and engineers. Some other students, however, opted for the decidedly smaller biology and chemistry stream, and these young people were generally thought of as the country's future candidates for medical school. Dana, Alex, and Dan had all completed their high school studies in the same class, within this stream.

In their last year of high school, students from the biology and chemistry stream were asked to complete a two-week-long apprenticeship at the Municipal Hospital in the capital, so they could get a brief preview of what a career in a medical field would be like. During this time, they were allowed to watch surgeries as well as autopsies. Witnessing an autopsy for the first time was expected to be challenging, and so, in anticipation of potential problems, some staff members from the hospital stood behind the high school students, just in case anyone fainted. Alex was stoic, but Dan found the experience particularly unpleasant. It seemed surreal to see the naked dead body of a person at close range, on the long metal table, and the pungent smell of formaldehyde emanating from the preserved cadaver made it hard to breathe in the poorly ventilated basement room. The lab technician in charge of the autopsy was completely unconcerned — he must have done this hundreds of times — as he removed the liver from the cadaver and weighed it in front of the stunned students.

"This is what an enlarged liver looks like," the technician said matter-of-factly. "Probably the result of years of alcoholism. We will look at the brain next."

As the technician wiped the saw with a wet cloth, Dan's legs felt rubbery and a dark screen seemed to be lowered over his eyes in the seconds before he passed out. Fortunately, Alex was close by, and he caught Dan just in time.

When Dan opened his eyes again, a few minutes later, an assistant was standing over him, lightly slapping his cheeks.

"There's always one in every bunch," said the technician. "It's lucky your colleague was there to catch you, because otherwise you would have hit your head on the concrete floor, and then you might have ended up on this table."

Dana was there as well, looking concerned, and, as he slowly stood up, Dan thought he was going to die of shame.

When he got home that evening, Dan told his parents what had happened, but his mother dismissed the incident as unremarkable.

"This is very common," she said. "When I first met your father, in our first year at the Faculty of Medicine, he used to pass out each time he saw blood. And look at him now — a surgeon at the Emergency Hospital."

Unlike most of his classmates, Alex was never really interested in medicine, and was in that academic stream because of his lifelong love of biology, which competed only with his passion for writing and literature for top spot among his career preferences. In other words, he saw the study of various aspects of biology as the ultimate goal, and not a mere stepping stone towards a medical degree. Most of his med school-bound colleagues appeared to think that only some type of character flaw or intellectual deficiency would prevent someone from choosing to become a doctor, but Alex did not care. He knew he was smarter than all of them, and he was immune to peer pressure.

Alex had been fascinated by the mysteries and intricacies of the living world as far back as he could remember, and he was collecting plants and bugs shortly after he had learned how to walk. During the summers of his childhood, his arms and legs were frequently covered by all sorts of insect bites, as he was busy exploring the tall grass and weed-covered fields near his home, looking for new species of beetles and butterflies. He learned to impress his friends with his ability to find and handle dangerous-looking bugs. After a while, he noticed that some insects left behind peculiar odors when bothered, and it dawned on him that these may be defensive mechanisms against enemies, such as spiders, small birds, or even nosy kids. Eventually, he figured out which insects were chemically protected from predators, and which ones were not, and he recorded his observations in a series of carefully catalogued notebooks.

At the age of ten, he received a small Japanese microscope, purchased by his father during a rare trip abroad, and this thoughtful gift opened up entire new worlds. Alex used his microscope to examine a sample of water and mud taken from the bottom of his aquarium, and was amazed by what he saw. Dozens of tiny living organisms of different shapes and colors, entirely undetectable by the naked eye alone, were swimming around and zipping by through his field of view. There was so much life in a single drop of water, and Alex asked himself how many types of minute forms of life may have been present in the entire aquarium, and in the small pond found in a nearby woodlot. A comparative study seemed to be in order. The examination of only one sample had already shown, conclusively, that his aquarium sheltered a lot more biodiversity than previously thought. Obviously, Fortesque was not alone in there after all. Alex wondered how much vital extra nutrition his catfish may have derived from the rich detritus at the bottom of the tank. Perhaps that was the secret of the fish's good health and longevity. He wanted to understand at least some of the interactions and relationships among the various previously unknown species his microscope had allowed him to see. Years later, while studying the history of scientific discoveries, Alex understood his revelation must have been similar to that of Anton van Leeuwenhoek, the first man to discover microscopic life, using a relatively simple home-made microscope almost three centuries earlier.

Although the high school biology classes were taught in a specialized lab, experiments were almost never undertaken and many interesting specimens remained perpetually locked away in an adjacent storage room. Occasionally, the students would be asked to perform routine tasks, such as dissecting a frog — an assignment Alex found both distasteful and unnecessary — but more challenging and imaginative studies — for instance, analyzing the vocal communication systems of living amphibians — were absent from the curriculum. There were so many worthwhile subjects to learn and explore in more depth, and yet they had to waste so much time with utter nonsense.

Alex became more and more interested in the lives of the early naturalists and explorers, and became familiar with the works of Darwin, Wallace, von Humboldt, Steller, and many others. His broad interests were not limited to the natural sciences, however. An avid reader, he had gone through hundreds of books of all kinds — which were fortunately readily available in his family's vast private library — and had written quite a few short stories and a couple of novels already. In fact, during his high school years, he had also launched an underground, satirical magazine, which, not surprisingly, proved to be much more popular among his peers than the boring yearly official school publication. Dan and Victor also contributed to Alex's magazine from time to time — Dan would occasionally add illustrations to Alex's stories and editorials, and Victor was in charge of coming up with new and original mathematical puzzles. Since they had no access to copiers of any kind, only one copy of each handwritten magazine issue was produced, and each reader would get to take the magazine home for one day.

Encouraged by the local success of the magazine, the three friends expanded their range of extracurricular activities and started to record some of the sketches they wrote on cassette tapes. From that point on, it was only a matter of time before they also formed a musical group. They started by recording a song called *Mindless Fever* — a spoof of a typical sample of disco music. Next, came the epic *Galactic Burp*, which was inspired by their shared interest in science fiction. Although satire remained the main focus, Alex, who wrote all the songs, also tried to come up with reasonably good and original music. Victor was a reliable bass player, who worked tirelessly on improving his technique, and Dan was a passable amateur drummer, but the heavy workload fell on Alex's shoulders, since, in addition to being the lead singer, he had to take care of all the guitar parts, including the solos. Sometimes, a quirky young engineer who took the stage name Johnny Roadkill — even though his real name was Adrian and he normally worked on the design and repair of urban sewage systems — helped out on rhythm guitar on the rare occasions when the band performed in a small club downtown. Once in a while, Gabriel would join them as well to contribute some brilliant piano playing, but they did not ask him often, since he was a great musician, and the contrast between his level of skill and theirs was just too embarrassingly big. Still, they improved over time, and Alex's wit and imagination made several songs of the group quite appealing to their small but growing fan base.

They had a tough time coming up with a name for their new band. Their first more accomplished song — one of Alex's favorites — was titled *Herd Mentality*, so Alex suggested they should call themselves The Ungulates, but the others disagreed, so eventually, after trying a few other self-deprecating names —The Nobodies, The Hopeless Amateurs, and The Bad Band — they settled on The Unspeakables, and stuck with that name for a while.

The truly reputable academic high schools left in the big city seemed concentrated in the downtown core for the most part. As a result, like many other students from the suburbs, Alex and Victor had to spend at least a couple of hours or so during each school day riding the capital's notoriously overcrowded and poorly maintained buses. This was often an adventure in and of itself. To begin with, it was not apparent that a formal bus schedule actually existed. The typical answer frustrated people could expect to get from a cornered public transport company official would be: "I don't know. Why are you asking me? Do I look like I have a crystal ball? It will come, when it will come."

And when the bus did eventually come, in the early morning, before the work day officially began, a restless crowd of frighteningly large proportions would be waiting, ready to pounce. There were obviously many more people in the station than could fit into any one bus, so being big and strong was clearly a major asset. Strategic positioning, and the ability to anticipate exactly where the bus doors would be when the bus finally stopped, were also essential for success. After that, the survival instincts took over. There was no room for compassion, hesitation, or squeamishness. It was crush-or-be-crushed time. The pushing and shoving were part of the daily workout. Sharp elbows and the willingness to put them to good use certainly helped. The buses were usually packed well beyond the maximum planned carrying capacity, and the doors could not close because of all the people standing on the steps and hanging on by their fingertips to the outer door frames for dear life. Alex was frequently one of those people. Aside from the constant risk of dying, for instance by falling under the big wheels, or getting hit by another vehicle nearby, riding with most of one's body protruding on the outside of the bus had its benefits. For one thing, the air quality was clearly better out there. Even taking in the traffic-caused pollution of the major streets at close range, while holding on to the open bus doors or other fellow passengers, was preferable to being hopelessly stuck inside, entirely unable to move, and barely able to breathe at all, among all sorts of similarly squashed, grim-faced and irascible strangers, some of whom had clearly not showered in a good long while. The conversations were better on the outer steps, as well, and a sense of easy camaraderie often developed among the riders brave enough to travel alfresco. Alex and Victor had insightful discussions with fellow passengers about the prospects of the local football teams or the action scenes in some new American cop shows on TV while riding this way. If you missed an episode of *Kojak* or *Mannix*, this was a good way to catch up.

The buses were of the articulated variety, which meant that they looked somewhat like oversized accordions and were prone to bizarre mishaps. While all public transit vehicles could break down from time to time, of course, articulated buses had the added distinction of being able to also break apart. Alex had actually experienced this first hand on a couple of occasions — once when he was going to school in the morning, and the other time when he was on his way to a birthday party downtown, on a Saturday evening. In the latter instance, the driver drove on for about a hundred meters or so, before some of the passengers pointed out to him that the posterior half of his bus had been left behind, stranded in the middle of the street. After finally stopping the bus, the driver walked back, scratched his head, and whistled in amazement, while looking at the remains of his bus.

"It's going to be one hell of a job putting this back together," he opined, as a crowd of onlookers was beginning to gather.

"Why would you want to?" someone in the crowd asked.

"Look, we have to drive something. I don't know why they give us this junk. I am not paid to ask questions," the driver answered.

For a while, Victor experimented with taking his bicycle to school, but this proved to be even more insanely dangerous than the bus rides. At that time, the concept of a bike lane was as foreign to the locals as the notion of a light bulb must have been to Neanderthals. Furthermore, many of the city's drivers could best be described as overly assertive, nothing to lose, thrill-seeking types, whose main purpose on the roads seemed to be never to let anyone else get in front of them at any cost. Besides, whenever he was forced off the road by some lunatic driver, and sustained minor injuries and damage to the bicycle, the police always used to pick on him — the innocent cyclist — and tell him to smarten up and stay off the main streets if he wanted to remain alive. In any event, Victor's final choice of modes of transportation was made for him, when his beloved and much repaired bicycle was stolen from the backyard of the high school. When he reported the theft, the principal yelled at him, and told him there was simply no room for bicycles on the premises.

"Did you ever consider what would happen if every student decided to bring his bike to school? Well? Where would I park my car? And where would we hold the outdoor school assemblies and ceremonies? There are one thousand other students in this school. You simply cannot be that selfish," the principal admonished.

Dan often avoided the daily discomfort of public transit because he was usually driven to school by his father, whose workplace was nearby, and Dana was a downtown girl who could see the high school from her apartment's balcony, and therefore did not need to worry about commuting.

10

On the evening when the big earthquake hit the capital, Dan was at his desk, in his room, doing his homework for the next day's English class. He was in grade eight at the time, and English was a relatively new subject in the curriculum. All of a sudden, the windows started rattling to an unbelievable extent and a big, unfamiliar roaring noise, like the imagined sound made by a huge mythical dragon, seemed to emerge from the bowels of the earth. A heavy bookshelf came crashing down behind him, missing him by just a few centimeters. Dan felt dizzy, as he ran towards the door, where his parents were waiting. Chunks of concrete were falling from the ceiling, and, as they opened the front door, they could hear people screaming.

Dan and his parents spent the night walking outside, in the park and the open fields near their building. As they walked, they ran into many neighbors — including Alex and his parents — who were doing the same thing, and they all talked excitedly to each other about what would happen next and when it would be safe to go back home. Normally, people think of their home as a refuge from dangers present outside, but this time, after the earthquake, the home had become a potential death trap. When he finally returned to his room, Dan had a tough time falling asleep. His father had tied a key to a string, and attached the string to the door handle, and Dan kept watching the key to see if it would swing from side to side in response to new vibrations.

In Dan's part of town, the buildings were fairly new, and so, although there was some damage, and he could put his entire hand through some of the cracks in the wall beside the staircase, there were no casualties. Unfortunately, many of the older houses downtown were much harder hit and some even collapsed completely, or partially. Dana's father was making a house call, as a favor to a friend whose child was sick with the flu, when the earthquake brought the house down. The sick child survived, but Dana's father did not.

11

In their first year Clinical Anatomy course, Dan and Dana were lab partners, and, as a result, they had to dissect a cadaver together over the course of several months. Dan was not very good with the scalpel, but Dana was better and had much steadier hands. They had decided to pair up for the lab sessions, mainly because they had known each other reasonably well since their high school days.

Although this was just about the least romantic setting possible, Dan saw the lab partnership as a golden opportunity, and, as they were analyzing the structure of the abdominal muscles on the cadaver, he finally summoned up the courage to ask Dana out. At first, she didn't seem to hear him, as she was concentrating on her dissection, but after he repeated himself, she looked up at him from behind her protective goggles, smiled, and, following an awkward moment of apparent hesitation, agreed.

At the end of the session, they removed their white lab coats, and walked across a green space on their way to a trendy coffee shop nearby. Dan thought this would be a nice, intimate place for a sort of informal first date, but things did not quite turn out as expected, because all the patrons and waiters in the small establishment kept staring in the direction of their table.

"What's the matter with them?" Dan whispered self-consciously to his date.

"I think it's probably the formaldehyde smell," said Dana, whose cheeks were beginning to turn slightly red. "We became used to it, but it persists on our clothes and makes us stand out in here. They probably think we stink."

12

The stern woman behind the giant desk packed with dust-covered boxes flipped through the thick file with obvious disgust, and then said:

"You don't have form XT 10034 B-12 in here. I cannot accept this until you bring that to me."

"Actually, the form is there," said Alex trying not to sound impatient.

"Where? I don't see it."

"Right behind form XT 10034 B-11. The two forms are stapled together."

"I see," said the bureaucrat looking as if she had just sucked on a particularly bitter lemon. "And who told you to staple these together?"

"You did, the last time I was here, two weeks ago," said Alex.

"I don't recall that," said the woman. "Now I'll have to remove the staple and replace it with a paper clip."

Do you think you would need another two weeks for that? Alex thought, but he didn't say anything.

"And why isn't this certificate submitted in triplicate?" asked the woman after a few minutes, with renewed hope.

"Because according to item number thirty-two on page fifteen of the list of instructions, this particular certificate should only be submitted in duplicate," said Alex, trying not to sound sarcastic. "But I have another copy, in case you need it," he added.

"No, that would not be necessary," said the woman. "In fact, I'll have to take and destroy that extra copy. There are not supposed to be any loose copies of the certificate — outside the file, that is." She was clearly unhappy that Alex had come prepared and the file seemed to be complete, and she looked like she had just attended a funeral.

Alex handed the additional copy to her and made a special effort not to comment.

"You looked different in the picture in your file," the woman observed.

"I was a lot younger when I started this application process," said Alex, no longer trying to suppress his sarcasm.

The woman took off her glasses and rubbed her eyes. She looked tired and defeated.

"I am only doing my job," she said. "It will take us a while to process all this. It may be quite some time before you'll get your passport and I have no control over that, but your file is now complete."

"I know," said Alex, and he turned towards the door to leave the office.

13

"I must admit that I don't envy your choice of friends," the colonel said, just before lighting up his customary after dinner cigarette. "Not one bit, to be frank about it. You are routinely associating with a young man who has formally asked to leave our country permanently and has been thrown out of the university as a result. This type of association is not only unwise — it is dangerous. You are judged by the company you keep. Just remember that." He then turned his back briefly, blowing smoke towards the thick gray curtains, and added some more wine to his nearly empty glass.

Victor looked at his future father-in-law in silence, and noticed how incredibly thick and reddish the military man's neck was. Every time he had wine, which was quite often, the colonel's face and neck got redder and his already foul mood got worse. He was usually mean even when sober, but alcohol made him meaner. Victor remembered Alex's whispered remarks, after meeting the colonel for the first time, during a party at Silvia's house: "How can she possibly be related to this nasty baboon? She is either adopted, or the milkman is the real father. So, either way, don't worry, because your kids won't have any of his genes." The sudden recollection made it impossible for Victor to suppress a very faint smile, but that only seemed to upset the colonel further.

"This is really no laughing matter. I must say I am surprised by your attitude. You can no longer think just of yourself. You have great responsibilities now. I am about to entrust you with the future of my only daughter. Don't make me regret it."

Victor remembered the times when Silvia had spoken to him about responsibilities, and their steady future together, and he suddenly felt sick, and in desperate need of fresh air.

14

The district where Alex lived was known as one of the better bedroom communities built largely in the 1960s and '70s. It was the type of rare neighborhood where people could actually own their new apartments, and this proved attractive to many of the slightly more affluent and established families in the capital at the time. Alex's parents had bought the apartment he was now living in, and had paid for it in full. However, after their departure for the West, the apartment was declared officially the property of the state. Alex was allowed to stay in the apartment, but, since his parents were considered to have "betrayed the motherland" by settling permanently in Canada, government bureaucrats decided that the apartment should now be listed as confiscated and no compensation would be given to either Alex or his family. Alex thought of challenging the absurd and arbitrary decision in court, but a lawyer who was a friend of the family advised him to drop the matter, since any further action could not have accomplished anything positive and would probably have resulted in Alex's eviction from the apartment and additional delays in the processing of his file and application to leave the country. A brand-new neighborhood had been added to the capital, and people were encouraged to move there and use their life savings for the purchase of rather small apartments, but property rights obviously meant nothing in their country, since the government could always take them away on a whim for virtually any reason. According to one of the several often-repeated slogans they were forced to endure, "Everything belongs to the people!" But in reality, everything belonged to the state, and especially to a few people at the top, who had their choice of fancy villas and cars and special shops, while everybody else struggled in this so-called "proletarian paradise." In fact, despite all the vile propaganda, their communist society was never egalitarian. That was just a myth meant to justify the take-over and fool the gullible and the naïve. The arrival of communism had simply replaced the previous ruling class with another one, made up of mostly semi-literate party activists.

Alex had covered almost the entire considerable distance — about 12 km or so — between the city center and his suburban apartment building on foot, and he was just looking at his watch to see how long the journey had taken, when the dogs came. It was almost 2 a.m., and there was no one else in the unlit and eerily quiet streets. Alex felt for a moment as if he had been unwittingly transported right into a recreation of one of Jack London's *Tales of The North*, except that this took place on a paved city street, in Europe, in the late twentieth century.

As the city kept expanding, surrounding villages were quickly demolished. Before they were forced to abandon their homes, the villagers often just set their dogs free. This was one of the more common explanations for the origin of the feral dog packs which roamed the suburbs at will. During the day, when people outnumbered the dogs, the risk of being bitten was relatively small, but at night, on the nearly empty streets, the hounds were in charge, and their residual fear of humans seemed to be dissipating. To make things worse, some of the dogs had not been treated very well by their former masters. A few of the older dogs still carried visible signs of past mistreatment, such as pieces of rusty broken chains wrapped tightly around their necks or the permanent scars of former beatings. The feral dog population had exploded over the years, and although there were no official counts, there must have been at least several hundred roaming Alex's district, and possibly many thousands loose in the entire city. The dogs were gradually reverting to a semi-wild state, forming packs which fought fiercely for control of territory and resources. Alex had often been awakened in the middle of the night by the primeval blood curdling sounds of dogs fighting each other or attacking cats, other smaller animals, and maybe, occasionally, even humans. Although this was not officially reported, stories emerged from time to time about people torn to shreds by packs of feral dogs — usually at night, and almost everybody seemed to know someone who had been bitten, maimed, or threatened by the dogs. Sometimes, people took matters into their own hands, and the results were usually gruesome. Alex remembered seeing about fifteen dead dogs — an entire pack — lying stiffly in the street among the garbage cans near his former elementary school, several years ago. As kids were leaving the school after classes, they stopped to look at the sad scene, made even more unsettling by the fact that many children actually knew the dogs and had even given them names. Since it seemed very unlikely that all these dogs would just happen to drop dead at the exact same time of natural causes, deliberate poisoning of the garbage looked like the most probable explanation for the mass slaughter. Alex had wondered who would be reckless enough to poison the garbage bins so close to a school.

And so, the dogs had learned to mistrust and even resent people, and the people had good reasons to fear the dogs.

As much as he admired the dogs' ability to survive on their own under harsh conditions, Alex also had to face his unenviable predicament, as he suddenly found himself followed by an entire large pack of perhaps twenty or twenty-five dogs. Only the toughest dogs could survive in the streets. There was no room for toy poodles here. All feral dogs were fairly big, and most were powerfully built and frequently hostile towards anyone perceived as an intruder in the territory controlled by their pack. And apparently, while walking home, Alex had stumbled upon such a well-guarded territory. He had the distinct feeling of being hunted. The dogs were following him from behind, and as they got closer, they suddenly split into two groups. One group, led by a big, scary-looking one-eyed dog, went through some bushes to the left of Alex, and the other group turned to his right, blocking his access to the door of the nearest apartment building. These doors were usually kept locked at night, and residents only had the key to their own apartment building, so this wouldn't have been a viable escape route in all likelihood anyway. Alex stopped in the middle of the street, and assessed his dwindling options. If only he had something he could use to defend himself — a tennis racquet, or a sturdy tree branch. Maybe even a rock, or some other type of projectile. Anything he could keep the dogs at bay with, or at least use to show his determination to fight hard for his life, and make a big impression on his would-be predators. There were no trees big enough to climb in this young neighborhood, and, in any event, the nearest tree — more of a shrub, really — emerged from among the dense bushes where several dogs were hiding. His own apartment building — visible at the end of the street — was still much too far away. Making a run for it would only make things worse. They would really hunt him then. And besides, the dogs were slowly forming a large circle around him, and in order to get to the apartment building he would have to walk right through them.

He remembered hearing that you could always tell if a deer was killed by wolves or dogs, because wolves killed quickly and efficiently, with a few well-placed bites, whereas dogs tended to bite everywhere, hundreds of times, before the prey finally died of its many injuries.

The big one-eyed dog — the unquestioned leader of the pack — advanced towards him cautiously, and Alex thought he could hear an incipient growl. Not a good sign, in other words. He thought about how ridiculous it would be to die here, in this supposedly safe and secluded suburban neighborhood, after surviving encounters with wild bears in the mountains and having emerged unscathed from the meeting with the secret policeman. So, it looks like I may not see Canada, after all, he thought, while his mind was racing, still trying to find a way out of this seemingly impossible situation.

And then the car came. The dogs backed off a bit, reluctantly, as the driver kept flashing the lights and honking the horn to scare them away. Alex watched, as the car window was rolled down and Dan's head suddenly appeared.

"You should have taken a cab," said Dan. "Get in before we both get killed."

"You know, for once I think I'm actually happy to see you," Alex replied with a relieved smile as he quickly entered the car and slammed the door shut rather hastily.

15

Standing in the middle section of an unusually empty articulated bus, on his way to his grandfather's house for one last visit before his departure, Alex noticed a uniformed policeman who was menacingly staring at him. Alex stood out, since he was tall, had long hair and a full beard, and was wearing genuine American-made blue jeans and a new Canadian winter coat sent over by his parents, with a small but conspicuous red maple leaf logo on the chest pocket located on the left side. It was an unusually mild day for the season, and the coat was made for the much tougher Canadian winters, so Alex kept it unbuttoned, revealing a T-shirt which showed an image of the Beatles from around 1969. Alex was well aware that his appearance was frowned upon by the authorities, who promoted a more tradi-tional proletarian look and were threatened by any obvious Western influences on the way local people dressed and expressed themselves. However, he was usually left alone, and resisted official attempts to make him conform and join what he called in his less generous moments "the mindless herd of spineless and compliant mediocrities."

The policeman's persistent stare was becoming a potential problem, and Alex sensed the cop was trying to decide whether to confront Alex about his unconven-tional look or not. This angered Alex, so he decided to seize the initiative. Since this clown seems to think I look too Western for this place, maybe I should just play the part and show him I'm not from around here, thought Alex, as he ad-vanced confidently towards the policeman.

"Excuse me, do you know if this bus is going to the Old Town?" said Alex in English to the now disoriented cop.

The gamble worked. The policeman's demeanor changed immediately, from threatening to stunned and helpless. All of a sudden, the policeman realized that he wasn't looking at a rebellious local youth, but at a foreign tourist, and that made an enormous difference. As Alex had suspected, the policeman couldn't speak English, and, furthermore, he was not allowed by law to speak to foreigners. All contacts with foreigners — particularly those from the West — had to be reported to the authorities, and this could lead to some uncomfortable questions and other complications. As a result, the policeman was now reduced to waving his arms defensively and mumbling incoherently, while backing away from Alex and waiting eagerly for the next stop so that he could escape this suddenly unbearable situation.

16

As Alex walked uphill along the narrow winding cobblestone street leading to his grandfather's home, he noticed that some of the old houses on the lower side of the slope had already been partially demolished, while others were still intact but had been abandoned and were awaiting imminent demolition. A few stray cats lingered among the ruins. The formerly vibrant neighborhood had been largely destroyed already. A wave of sadness mixed with nostalgia swept over Alex as he recalled childhood memories tied to this area. Before moving to the newly built district in the faraway West End of the capital at the age of ten, Alex had lived in an apartment located within easy walking distance of his grandfather's house.

During that time, every year on Christmas Eve, Alex's father was left alone in the apartment to put up and decorate the Christmas tree, while Alex and his mother walked over to the grandfather's house nearby and waited there eagerly for the phone call that would inform them Santa Claus had arrived, and therefore it was now safe to return home and open the gifts. Santa was always generous, but could never be seen delivering the many gifts for some reason. Apparently, he was a publicity-shy mystery man who did not like to receive thanks for his good deeds directly.

In Alex's country, Santa Claus was known as Old Man Christmas, but the communists tried to replace that name with Old Man Frosty. However, the attempted change did not catch on, and the original name remained popular.

Alex remembered the 1969 Christmas, when he was in grade one. On the little Russian-made, black-and-white TV set in his home, he watched and greatly enjoyed *The Magnificent Seven* western with Yul Brynner and Steve McQueen for the first time. A pleasant smell of homemade baked pies came from the kitchen, carols could be heard outside, and among the nice gifts he received there was his first postage stamp album and toys that looked just like Disney's seven dwarfs.

Alex remembered taking a long look at those toys in the window of a store just a few weeks earlier, during a walk with his father, and was very pleased to see them under the Christmas tree on that day. Somehow, Santa was a mind-reader, and knew exactly what Alex wanted to get each Christmas. That was a good memory of a nice day.

17

Alex's grandfather was a brilliant man. Fluent in five languages, he had a doctorate from the Sorbonne, and had also studied at Oxford and Heidelberg. He had produced some of the very first detailed studies and surveys of his country's cave inhabiting species, and was a world-renowned authority on freshwater crustaceans and fish, and a trail-blazer in the field of biogeography. Before the war, when this was still possible, he had participated in international expeditions to faraway places, bringing his contribution to exciting discoveries of new forms of life. At the last count, there were at least ten species of crustaceans and five species of fish named in his honor by grateful colleagues. His list of scientific publications was impressive, particularly when taking into account the premature end of his academic career, due to his perceived political dissent, and he had been an inspiring and highly respected professor, widely loved and admired by his students.

But the grandfather's health had been declining for some time, and he was never the same after his release from detention. In the last few years, his once prodigious memory started to fade as well. At first, this was hardly noticeable — just a perfectly understandable failure to recall a name or a face — but lately, the problem had gotten worse, and he was often having problems remembering people and events he used to know so well. The grandfather was still a very perceptive and intelligent man, and he was usually aware of his limitations, and even joked about his fading memory from time to time, in an attempt to hide his embarrassment and discomfort.

There were good days and bad days, and, as he entered the grandfather's beautiful house for possibly the last time, to say goodbye, Alex felt the weight of the occasion and found himself wondering what type of day this would turn out to be.

The kind and devoted housekeeper who was taking care of his grandfather greeted him at the door with a warm smile, and took his coat.

"How is he today?" Alex whispered, and the housekeeper smiled again and answered, rather ambiguously:

"As well as can be expected, under the circumstances."

The news of Alex's imminent departure had been communicated and explained to his grandfather already, in anticipation of this visit, but nobody could be quite sure how the old man would react or even if he fully understood the situation.

His grandfather never made any attempt to hide the fact that Alex was by far his favorite relative. He was always in Alex's corner, and whenever there was even the slightest possibility of a disagreement on the horizon, the old man did his best to adjust his views and try to see things from Alex's perspective.

"You must forgive a stubborn old gent, stuck in his ways," he used to say, but there was nothing to forgive.

Alex felt selfish for hoping that this last meeting would not in any way tarnish the many good memories he had of his grandfather. He desperately wanted everything to go well, and wasn't sure if he could find a way to break through the awkwardness of the moment. And most of all, he wanted his real grandfather back — the way he used to be before the cruel illness started to take him away.

But Alex needn't have worried. Once again, his grandfather found a way to rise to the occasion, as he had done so many times before. The old man woke up very early that morning, in anticipation of the important visit. He had showered and put on his best clothes, and then rummaged through closets and big boxes for a long time. The housekeeper thought something might be wrong, and offered to help out, but the grandfather had a plan and did not need any assistance.

He had collected old family photographs and documents and had spread them in chronological order on the big table in the dining room for Alex to see. Alex saw many of the items on display for the very first time, and he felt both grateful and relieved to see his grandfather in such good form, and so close to his very best. The old man spoke passionately and eloquently. He showed the teaching certificate of his mother — Alex's great grandmother — the first female teacher in her home town, and pictures of his brothers — one of whom was killed in the war, on the eastern front, while the other was shot by the communists after the war, when

he refused to surrender his beloved horses to the authorities during the collectivi-
zation process — and told vivid and poignant stories and anecdotes of days gone
by. The grandfather spoke of everyone's accomplishments but his own.

"You must forgive me for talking so much, but I am not sure when we'll talk
again, and I have so much to tell you," he said.

"We will talk again, grandfather," said Alex, trying to sound hopeful.

"I just want you to remember, because I soon won't be able to. I don't know if
I said it before, but I want you to know I am very proud of you."

And for the first time in their lives, the two men briefly embraced.

18

Near an open-air market where farmers brought their products, Alex observed a shabbily dressed old lady sitting on the cold pavement, with a little torn mat in front of her. On the mat, there were just a handful of oddly shaped vegetables, with many obvious flaws. It seemed clear that the unappetizing-looking vegetables had been discarded by other farmers, and the old lady had collected them and now tried to sell them herself, to make a little money. Alex was impressed by the dignified appearance of the elderly woman, and he was deeply touched by the scene he was witnessing. The old lady could have chosen to beg, like some other down-on-their-luck people in that neighborhood, but, instead, she tried to offer something, however small, in return for the money.

Unfortunately, she did not seem to have any success at selling anything, and she just sat there, quiet and sad looking, as the passers-by simply ignored her. That bothered Alex. It bothered him a lot. He was surprised by just how upset he really felt. He tried to walk away, but couldn't get far. And so, he returned, stopped in front of the old woman, and asked her, as politely and pleasantly as he could, how much the vegetables on display would cost. The frail old lady looked up at him cautiously, clearly surprised, and wondered which of the vegetables Alex was thinking of buying.

"All of them, please, if possible," said Alex.

"Are you sure, sir?" she asked shyly, and he confirmed his request.

She asked for a very small sum of money — just a pittance, really, but he offered much more.

"Are you sure?" she asked again, and he said yes — he was quite sure, and he collected the vegetables, put them in the small backpack he was carrying, gave her the money, and thanked her for everything.

"Thank you, sir. Thank you very much. You are a very kind man, and I wish you good luck," she said.

Alex thought he could detect a little spark of gratitude and recognition in her aging eyes. He felt temporarily soothed and healed by that look, and so he thanked her again.

19

On his way to meet his friends, Dan drove by his former girlfriend's apartment building, downtown, and felt overwhelmed by deep regret — the kind of regret that could generate physical pain. He remembered one of their last meetings, towards the end of their rather brief and unhappy relationship. They were talking about Alex's upcoming departure — Dan had just found out Alex had applied for a passport and was sharing the news, and Dana seemed upset, although she was trying to pretend to be indifferent. However, her feigned indifference quickly turned to anger, as she chose to focus on Alex's selfishness.

"I am not worried about him," she said coldly. "He will go far, since he never has to carry the burden of caring about others."

"That's not quite fair," Dan heard himself reply. "I've known him for most of my life, and he can be a bit abrasive sometimes, but I think we both know he is a good man."

"Don't tell me what I know," said Dana.

"I was just trying to…" Dan began, but she cut him off and gave him a hurt look.

"I don't think you'll ever understand me," she concluded and then walked into another room closing the door behind her.

Dan stood alone in the lobby of Dana's apartment for some time, feeling embarrassed. What motivated him to stand up for a friend whose place he was trying to take in Dana's heart? Why couldn't he just shut up and go along? Was he subconsciously trying to sabotage his relationship with Dana? Why did he even bring up the recent news about Alex? Dana could have found out from someone else, surely, and then any predictable arguments would have been avoided. Why couldn't he just talk about something neutral and safe, like the weather or his grandmother's passion for knitting, instead? Was he feeling guilty about trying to win Dana's affection while Alex was still in town? Did she think he was surreptitiously testing her by talking about potentially painful subjects to see how she would react? Was he expected to take sides and choose between an old friend and a new girlfriend? Was that fair? Why did every mention of Alex's name, no matter how casual, lead to an argument? Dan kept thinking and analyzing and he felt overwhelmed by all the possibilities. Was he not allowed to talk about a childhood friend anymore? What other topics could become off limits in the future? Did he rush things a bit too much? Perhaps he should have been more patient. Waiting until Alex finally left the country may have been wiser, but then others may have tried to move in. There was no shortage of would-be Casanovas among their fellow medical students, and even an old professor or two were taking an unseemly interest in Dana.

Dan tried to be supportive and kind, but Dana rarely seemed to reciprocate and try to understand how he felt, for a change. She used her unhappiness as a shield, and an excuse to keep him at a comfortable distance. He wanted to be considered a real boyfriend and not just a compassionate flower delivery man. He hated to be told he was a nice guy, in a way that suggested being nice was a limitation he couldn't overcome. He felt Dana was treating him unfairly by never responding enough to his efforts to make things better — to help her move on and be happier. Perhaps she was really the selfish one, after all, and was too wrapped up in her own problems to notice that he had feelings, concerns, and opinions, as well. He wished he could be tougher, the way Alex was. Dan believed everyone deserved a genuine love story, and, as he left her apartment that day, he started to think that perhaps he could never experience that with Dana.

And then, as he was wrestling with all these questions and doubts, an older memory came back to him. It was another embarrassing incident. Students whose birthdays fell on particular school days sometimes brought a box of chocolates to class, and gave a piece of candy to each of their colleagues and their teachers. It was a nice gesture, of course, and also a good way to avoid being examined on that day. When his birthday came along, Dan followed this tradition, but he did not realize that there were not enough pieces of chocolate in his box for everybody in the class. Somehow, he had miscounted, and that was one of the rare days when everybody showed up for classes. Nobody was sick and no one was away. Dan was turning purple, standing there with an empty box in his hand, facing several classmates who did not receive any chocolates, and not knowing what to do next, when Alex, who was in the same class, saved the day, by standing up and starting to sing "Happy Birthday" with his booming voice. Pretty soon everyone was standing and singing and this allowed Dan to retreat to his bench and save face to some extent. The embarrassing moment had passed, thanks to Alex and his presence of mind.

20

Alex was required to check his luggage at the airport well in advance — at least twenty-four hours before his departure, so that the security personnel would have plenty of time to go through his bags with extreme care and make sure he abided by the regulations. The list of rules was long: no handwritten documents or texts of any kind, no photo albums — presumably because someone could have written secret messages on the back of the photographs before gluing them on to the album pages, no books published before 1945 (the year when the communists took over the country), no foreign books, no tapes, no films, no unauthorized documents, nothing framed (since there was no telling what could be hidden behind a frame), and so on. Alex thought about the idiocy of many of the restrictions. He didn't need to write any secret messages in notebooks or on the back of old family photographs — his memories were intact, and he could start writing them down as soon as he went beyond the borders of the country. And why would they prevent him from taking western-published books to the West? It all seemed pointless and ridiculous, just like so many other official policies, but this was also clearly punitive. They were determined to make things as unpleasant and difficult as possible until the very end. They wanted the few people fortunate enough to be able to leave for a better life to go away without many of their most treasured possessions — the few things they could not replace, such as photographs of loved ones.

Alex was leaving with one big suitcase and a small carry-on bag. His other possessions would have to stay behind, and had already been distributed among a few friends and relatives. Months before the anticipated departure, he had started to mail some of the books from his family's valuable library to his parents in Canada. He had to show identification and was only allowed to mail one package of books at a time, and that package could not weigh more than 5 kg. To speed things up, he enlisted the help of several friends and relatives, since each adult could mail a separate 5 kg package. This became a way for his friends to show their support, and, at one time, ten different people had accompanied him to the post office to help transport at least a part of this famous personal library across the ocean. "Our loss will be Canada's gain," said Dan, with a sad smile, while patting Alex on the shoulder, after doing his share by mailing some of the books.

And still, despite these valiant efforts, most of the books — including all the forbidden ones, of course — and all of Alex's meticulously catalogued notebooks, and the vast majority of the personal souvenirs and mementoes he had gathered with such enthusiasm and preserved so carefully over the years had to be abandoned. Alex found this both painful and unfair, although the idea that some of his belongings would go to people he liked — his treasured acoustic guitar, for example, was given to a young cousin who was just learning how to play that instrument — made the difficult situation a bit easier to tolerate. In his darker moments, Alex thought about the irony of his predicament. Most of his acquaintances seemed to envy him, and believed he was very lucky, even though he had been kicked out of university, had lost his home, and was leaving behind most of his possessions and almost everyone he ever knew, including all his friends, his former girlfriend, and all but two of his relatives.

Victor and Dan agreed to accompany Alex to the airport on the day before his flight, when he had to surrender his luggage to the authorities for a close inspection. They were there as witnesses, just in case, since Alex had heard about people in his situation who had been framed at the last minute, when stolen watches had been slipped into their pockets by undercover policemen. In fact, Alex had been advised by acquaintances with some experience with such matters to sow his pockets shut, and always hold the metal bar above his head with both hands while riding public transit buses. Of course, Victor and Dan couldn't have done anything to stop any such unfortunate events from happening — if the authorities really wanted to, they could have framed any of them at any time — but they came along mostly to show moral support, and also for another chance to spend a bit of time with their friend, before his departure. Besides, they were all planning a final get-together that evening at a favored downtown bar and ice cream parlor (a strange combination indeed), and so meeting a few hours early for a detour to the airport seemed like a logical thing to do. Furthermore, Dan, whose parents were affluent, was the only one who had his own car, and therefore he could drive them all first to the airport and then to the city center, where the Continental Bar was located.

The country's largest airport was a few kilometers away from the capital, in a rural area, and there were usually relatively few international flights coming and going each day, so not many passengers were around at any given time. Since Dan had to wait by the car, concerned about the safety of his vehicle, Victor was the only one who accompanied Alex to the security personnel area.

"What are you doing here? You're not supposed to be here!" a hostile policeman yelled at them.

"I'm leaving the country tomorrow. This is my passport. I am supposed to leave my bags here, today," said Alex, well aware that, when communicating with simpletons, it was best to keep the sentences short and clear.

The policeman looked at every page of Alex's passport carefully, with deep suspicion, as if he had never seen a passport before, and then waved him through, before turning to Victor and asking: "What about you?"

"I'm with him," said Victor, taken a bit by surprise.

"What do you think this is, a public promenade? Up against the wall!" ordered the policeman.

Alex walked through the squeaky doors of the secure area, while Victor had his face pressed against the dirty wall and was being thoroughly and roughly searched by the policeman.

On a wide desk, in the windowless room behind the doors, a large, balding official in a cheap blue suit rummaged through Alex's personal belongings with a disgusted look on his face. The ashes from the officer's cigarette were falling over Alex's folded shirts and pants. An unfinished ham and cheese sandwich was left on a filthy chair beside the table. I hope he sits on it after this is over, thought Alex, while wondering which items in his luggage the overzealous imbecile with greasy hands would pick on next.

Sure enough, just a few minutes later, the official took a couple of beautiful small paintings from Alex's suitcase. One showed an idyllic countryside setting with mountains in the background, and the other one was an old family portrait. The unframed oil paintings were original works by Alex's grandmother — an accomplished teacher and artist, who had died when Alex was only two years old. The official unwrapped the plastic and cardboard covers around the paintings rather roughly, stared moronically, and then asked derisively: "Who played with crayons, here? Was it you?"

Alex did not answer him, and resisted the impulse to forcefully remove the burning cigarette from the officer's big mouth and extinguish it between the nosy idiot's bulging toad-like eyes.

In the end, things did not go too badly. Alex was only asked to take back a few trinkets, deemed "unacceptable" for unspecified reasons, but the vast majority of the possessions he chose to take with him were officially approved.

As he walked back into the general public waiting area, Alex found a flustered and quite agitated Victor.

"I can't believe they confiscated my Swiss army knife," Victor said, angrily. "It was a gift from my father, and my name was engraved on it. I had it with me on all our mountain hiking trips."

"What did you expect? This is what these bastards do. They steal," said Alex.

"Not only that, but afterwards, the son of a bitch who took my penknife laughed in my face and said I shouldn't be playing with dangerous toys. And then he asked me if I was planning a career in tennis and whether I wanted to copy John Newcombe or Ion Țiriac with my handlebar mustache," Victor explained, still mad and incredulous.

"You should have told him you grew your thick mustache because you were trying to look more like his mother," suggested Alex.

But Victor was too upset to be appeased by a bit of humor. "The son of a bitch just laughed in my face. And there was nothing I could do about it," he said, red-faced, while staring at a soldier who was sleeping on a bench at the end of the corridor with a rifle by his side.

21

The bar of the Continental Hotel still looked pretty much the same as it must have appeared at the time of its opening, about one hundred years earlier. The three main crystal chandeliers hanging over the dozen or so small, elegant tables, the spotless giant mirrors on the walls, the old paintings showing mainly flowers and long-gone city landmarks, and the always silent grand piano near the entrance created the comforting impression of a refuge from the dreary modern times which had ravaged much of the surrounding urban landscape.

Located not far from the University and the National Theater, the bar had traditionally attracted both students and young actors, who liked to huddle there, despite the inflated prices such a sumptuous setting would demand. The ice cream — easily the best in the city — and the opportunity to sip real coffee, as opposed to the vile murky substitutes other establishments peddled, were just as attractive as the interior and the chance to look outside across the street and not see one single crane or huge hole in the ground. Almost no one came there for the alcohol.

There were exceptions, however. On the day Alex, Victor and Dan met at the Continental for the farewell coffee, ice cream, and cake, a hulking, surly figure was leaning heavily against the bar, occasionally moving the empty liquor glasses in front of him around, for no other apparent reason than to keep boredom at bay. There was nobody else in the establishment, except for the nervous-looking bartender, who seemed to vanish in a little back room at every opportunity. The atmosphere was further tarnished by the unsuitable music — a collection of the worst excesses of the disco era — which oozed from the speakers and took over the room like an oil slick.

Despite all this, Alex was determined to enjoy himself, and he had four scoops of ice cream — each of a different flavor — to prove it.

"My pre-cake snack," he beamed.

"Take it easy. You're flying tomorrow," said Victor, with his eyes fixed on the stranger at the bar.

"Who knows when I'll get to taste such fine ice cream again."

"Remember, you're going West, not East."

"I'm going to miss your wisdom, Vittorio."

It turned out to be the last good-natured remark of the evening, because then, all of a sudden, their farewell get-together was rudely interrupted by a coarse drunken voice, belonging to the heavy man at the bar.

"All you assholes ever do is talk. Blah-blah-blah... All day long. Useless talk. Nonsense talk. Stupid talk. You lazy, good-for-nothing sons of bitches are all talk. Worthless punks. Perhaps, I should shut you all up right now. Whaddya say to that?"

"Ignore him," said Victor, looking intently at the floor. "He's wearing a government issued suit, and there's a walkie-talkie in his coat pocket."

But the man at the bar got up, and was now shouting and advancing unsteadily towards their table.

"You, the one with the beard, I know all about you, you smug stupid bastard! You think you're so clever, but you're *not*! You're nothing! A nobody... I know all about you — I know you better than you know yourself! I got to know your friend, too. The music man. He liked to travel too much, just like you, you no-good punk, and he lost his voice, just like you will one day. I couldn't hear a peep out of him, by the time I was through. Got what he deserved — what you all deserve, you stinking, lousy parasites. I can take you out, one by one, until there are none of you left. You never have the guts to do anything. All you can do is talk among yourselves, and you think you have it all figured out. But you know nothing, and you can't do anything but talk. Blah-blah-blah... I'm so sick of listening to your nonsense. So sick and tired of all of you. Useless sons of bitches! You're all talk out here in the open... You..."

His voice trailed off, stifled by drink and surprise, as he watched Alex suddenly get up and step forward.

Through an open door, a piano could be heard from an apartment across the street. Somebody was giving lessons. Advanced ones. Beethoven, of course. A gifted student was learning his craft, perhaps a concert pianist in the making. Alex remembered Gabriel's last recital. It was Christmas Eve, and the concert hall was unheated. The audience members shared blankets and the musicians had to play with their overcoats on. During the short breaks between the festive pieces, Gabriel tried to keep his fingers warm by blowing hot air into his fists. Despite the numbing cold, everyone stayed until the very end, united by their love of music and their defiance of the demeaning conditions. They all gave Gabriel a standing ovation that night, the public and the other musicians alike. Even the crusty old conductor was clapping, with his baton securely placed under one arm. It was the last time Alex could remember seeing Gabriel really happy and proud.

Dan was very pale and felt suddenly glued to his chair, while Victor tried to think of something calming to say, but the events were overtaking him, and he felt a familiar warmth rising to his temples and spreading to his forehead.

Alex straightened his long back slowly and looked right at the corpulent man in the ugly brown suit. For a moment, a very long moment, only the labored breath of the fat man could be heard, as he assessed the naked hatred and infinite disdain in the young man's cold, hard stare. Then, the fat man spoke again, slightly slurring his scornful words, but Alex did not hear him.

The happy thoughts of the great upcoming trip and the delicious taste of the four scoops of ice cream were replaced by the recollection of the bear in the forest. This time, there could be no thoughts of retreat. No matter what. There was a small cross on a lonely mountain faraway, in the spot where a good man — an innocent, talented man, with a barely healed broken jaw and permanently damaged fingers — had fallen. Clever commentary and witty remarks in future articles and novels would never be enough to make up for that. Or for all the people who had to leave this place, in one way or another, forced out by the lowlife currently in charge. Was it worth moving ahead at the cost of always moving away? What good was self-preservation, if it always led to retreat? To a life spent on the run, always backing away from the fights that should not be avoided.

This opportunity would never come again. Perhaps he couldn't change the world, not right away, in any case, but he certainly could try to rearrange this monster's features. Alex knew this test had to be passed, not simply for the sake of primal, long-awaited revenge, but mostly so that he could live with the memory of this evening. He imagined the big man's heavy boot stepping on Gabriel's fingers, again and again. He wanted to crack the torturer's jaw in a million places — pulverize it, turn it to dust, and spread that dust all over the room. At that moment, nothing else seemed to matter.

And so, Alex advanced. Coldly and calmly, he stepped forward, feeling his muscles tightening in anticipation. He was surprised at how detached he really felt. He had often thought about what it would be like to face off against the bulky torturer, whose repulsive breath poisoned the room. Now, he was about to find out, and the uncertainty filled him with a strange excitement. He hadn't been trained to fight, but he was naturally strong and agile, and he believed he could win. He had always suspected that secret policemen were cowards at heart — lowly, inadequate, subterranean creatures of the dark, who were not accustomed to fair fights in public places. Let's see how this cockroach will do now, when he's not facing somebody tied to a chair, Alex thought to himself, as he prepared to deliver a devastating first blow.

The rock-hard punch came quickly, exploding against the square jaw and toppling the heavy body of the policeman over one of the small tables, which promptly broke in two under the unbearable weight. Alex turned around, just as surprised as the policeman must have been in the fraction of a second before Victor struck.

"It couldn't be helped," Victor said slowly, standing over the enormous motionless body on the floor, and looking past Alex, at the darkening sky visible through the large open door. Then, he turned towards Dan and added: "Just make sure he gets to the airport on time tomorrow morning. It would be a shame to miss that flight."

22

The airplane finally broke free from the short runway. As he double-checked his already fastened seatbelt, Alex glanced through the little oval window at a dwindling border guard, who was dancing in place to keep warm, in the shadow of an obsolete small airplane, permanently grounded in a nearby field. The country's biggest international airport looked tiny and provincial. As the aircraft struggled to gain altitude, the once proud capital below looked like nothing more than a gathering place for a grotesque assortment of rusting giant cranes. An enormous, nightmarish construction site for a perpetually unfinished monument to a mad ruler's restless tastelessness and unchecked power.

From the air, the people looked smaller and smaller, identical and insignificant, before disappearing completely, together with their houses and all remaining possessions, behind a thick blanket of gray winter clouds.

To amuse the passengers and help pass the time, the stewardess arranged a little contest, and asked everyone to estimate the length and wingspan of the aircraft in writing. The small pieces of paper from the hundred or so travelers were then scrutinized and compared. Naturally, Alex's estimate was the closest to reality (only about half a meter off on the wingspan, and just right on the length), and so he won the first prize — a bottle of German champagne — and the applause of his good-natured fellow passengers.

Fifteen hours later, after a stopover in Zürich, he would land at Mirabel Airport in Montreal. The temperature outside was -31°C, a snowstorm was approaching, and a bitter bus drivers' strike paralyzed the city. His brand-new life was about to begin.

Acknowledgements

I would like to thank my parents, Ileana and Silviu Guiaşu, for their constant support and encouragement throughout my life. My parents provided the opportunities for many fascinating intellectual explorations and rewarding outdoor activities, including hiking through the woods, mountain climbing, and visits to natural history museums and zoological and botanical gardens, throughout my Romanian childhood. I was fortunate to grow up in a household where so many wonderful books of all kinds were always available, and this stimulated my lifelong love of reading and writing.

My long-time partner, Doris Wong, spent countless hours discussing aspects of my work with me and showed unflinching support throughout my graduate studies and various stages of my academic career. Doris shares my love of nature and the great outdoors and has accompanied me on many wonderful hiking journeys in Europe and North America.

The following list of friends who joined me on mountain climbing and hiking trips may be incomplete, but should certainly include, in alphabetical order: Vlad Bînă, Valentin Ciurel, Ştefan Jianu, Adrian Leu, Victor Manolovici, Eugen Susanu, and Sorin Vlad (for making the journeys through the Carpathians of Romania memorable), and Bruce Barrett, Donald Collier, Eva Derka, Tuhin Giri, Spencer Mukai, Julie Ray, and Sharon Tomlinson (for helping me explore aspects of the vast Canadian wilderness). Best wishes to all.

I am grateful to everyone at Histria Books who contributed to the publication of this novel. I would like to thank, in particular, Diana Livesay (Assistant Director) for the always helpful and timely advice and guidance throughout the complex process of preparing the book for publication, Dana Ungureanu (Acquisitions Manager) for the encouraging early correspondence leading to the acceptance of the manuscript and the tireless work for the promotion of the novel, and Emily Schlick (Editor) for the insightful comments and careful analysis which led to improvements in the text.

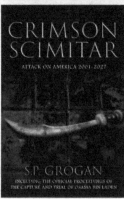